STRINGS

SARIPALLI VENKATA RAVI KIRAN

INDIA • SINGAPORE • MALAYSIA

ISBN 979-8-88869-960-7

ravikiransaripalli123@gmail.com

Phone: 9619192295

Hyderabad, India.

In fond memory of my father

Late Sri S V N DwarakaNath

who had sown the seed of story writing in me

In the second week of March 2021, my first cousin, Sri Padmasola Anil Kumar contacted me. He asked me to write a story revolving around the Coronavirus lockdown incidents.

The 'total lockdown' was clamped in India on 24th and 25th midnight March 2020 to mitigate the spread of CoronaVirus in the country.

Anil said he had a desire to shoot a short film based on an imaginary story around lockdown incidents.

When I began to weave the story, the characters plotted multiple twists.

By the time the antagonist was caught by the police, I have realised I have completed writing my first novel!

I love Anil to read the novel!

CONTENTS

Chapter 1

PAYAL, BHAGI AND SAHITHI COMPLEX

It was midnight!

Payal, 25 years young, was walking in the middle of a dense forest. The sky was brightly shining with white silver radiance of the full Moon. The forest was thickly covered with imposing Banyan and luxuriously vegetated Mahogany trees. The sparkling moon light was grappling hard to make its way through the canopy of the towering trees, their hazily woven leaves and branches. Tiny specks of silver-coloured light streaks pierced through the dark landscape evoking ghostly images all around.

Payal was a fearless and youthful soul. Yet, she was finding the going tough. Nervousness and anxiety declared a war and were contending to seize and win her over.

The obscure shadows were undulating in several sizes. She strived to comfort herself and was now trudging fast. Nocturnal species like owls were in a celebratory frame of mind when the backdrop was picture-perfect to thrill their senses. They were screaming, hooting, blaring and guffawing loudly. Bats were hanging upside down the branches, swaying menacingly. Packs of foxes and wolves were howling, staring at the sky.

She had to perform in a music concert and she was late!

She spotted a cave. It was looking dark and grave and had a narrow entrance.

She kept the guitar on her side, crawled in and examined. When she sneaked into the cave and was vigilantly watching its background, there had fallen a large boulder closing the entrance of the cave behind her.

She was trapped like a bee in a Tulip flower with its petals closed all over the bee. She was frightened. She yelled "Help! ...Help! ...Help! "

Payal woke up with a jolt.

She found herself comfortably in her bedroom-cum-music studio room in the 5th floor of Sahithi Luxury Gated Community, Madhapur, Hyderabad. The community was popularly known as 'Sahithi Complex.'

"Oomph. It's a dream ...", she muttered to herself.

She promptly moved her gaze towards the guitar and the electronic keyboard.

A large calendar with a life size picture of Jimi Hendrix, the legendary guitar player and songwriter, was dangling on the wall.

She glanced at the graduation certification which she received from Curtis Institute of Music, Pennsylvania, USA.

It was hung on the wall securely mounted inside a gilt-edged frame.

Her eyes shifted toward the laptop, the microphones, the synthesisers and the digital audio workstation.

Every gadget which inspired her to live a defined life was intact.

She felt assured.

It was 6.30 a.m. on 12th March 2020.

She got out of the bed, walked over to the window and pushed the curtains sideways.

Whenever she looked at the window curtains, her heart would surge with a sense of gratitude to Sneha – her '*Bhabi*'. Sneha was wedded to Daulat Ram, brother of Payal, seven years ago.

Daulat was running the sweets business by name "Mathura Sweets' - a retail chain of outlets of sweets, snacks and savoury in the twin cities of Hyderabad and Secunderabad. 'Mathura Sweets' was founded more than three decades ago by the forefathers of Daulat. Daulat had urged Payal to assist him in the business. Payal did not agree. She had a dream to go abroad and join a reputed music college; she had a plan to set up her own music production company in India. Daulat did not agree.

It was Sneha who prevailed over her husband to help Payal pursue a career in music.

Payal was a rebel at home. She had a boyfriend by name Mr. Sankar who was an Assistant Superintendent of Police. Daulat did not have a credible opinion about the police. That was another reason for him to dislike his sister!

Payal stood at the window. She could see a young woman swimming in the pool. The pool was located among the lawns adjacent to the club house.

A wave of cacophonous noise distracted her.

She found outside the compound wall more than a dozen women brawling with one another for a pot of drinking water in front of a municipal corporation water tanker.

She alternated her eyes between the sight of a glorious street fight for a pot of drinking water and a young woman who was floating alone on a large swathe of swimming pool like a pink flamingo on a lagoon.

'What a contrast!' she smiled away wistfully.

She recalled the song their unit was working on. She began to hum the tune. She reached out to the guitar. Her fingers brushed the strings of the guitar softly as she played a meditative tune.

She felt like savouring hot coffee. The time was nearing 7 a.m.

*****

Payal half opened her bedroom door and peeped into the living room.

Five people lived in that spacious four-bedroom grand luxury apartment.

Daulat Ram, his wife Sneha, their 6-year-old son, Bhagawat fondly called Bhagi, 60-year-old mother of the two siblings- Vasundhara and Payal resided in the flat.

Daulat's voice humming sweet words like, "my sweet pumpkin, lovely bunny, sweetie, honey, cutie potato, juicy mango" was floating in the air mollycoddling Bhagi!

Payal grasped that Bhagi must have sat on his dad's lap and was watching the cartoon network on the TV.

Daulat Ram would go daily at 5 a.m. to the central kitchen to personally inspect the activities, cheer up the employees and at the end invariably admonish the manager.

He would return home at 6.30 a.m.

He would then ease up on the couch, endearing his son for a couple of hours before he would step out to overlook the sales at the cash counters of the retail outlets spread across the twin cities.

Bhagi would grab the occasion to climb on to his dad's lap. He would sit with one *laddu* in the right hand and another *laddu* in the mouth. He would keep one hand empty to help balance himself on his dad's bouncy lap.

His mouth was always studded with one sweet or the other. It was the reason why the timbre quality of Bhagi's voice was not known to anyone. His posture, when he sat on his dad's lap, was close in resemblance to the posture of *Modaka Khadika*.

Bhagi's rotund belly and bubbly cheeks would prompt any worldly and mundane soul to hold and yank his soft cheeks and affectionately fondle a gentle blow into the belly.

Payal looked around for Sneha.

Sneha must be having intuition as her first guiding factor. She was expecting Payal to appear at the bedroom doorway. From nowhere, she came and handed a cup of coffee to Payal and said, "Hi! Good morning."

Payal greeted," Good morning, *Bhabi*."

Sneha shouted, "Bhagi, come on… school time is up. Driver Raju is waiting. Come for a bath."

Driver Raju was waiting at the entrance doorway of the flat. He was neatly dressed in a white uniform.

Daulat heard Sneha's voice. He also urged Bhagi to take a bath.

Bhagi slithered down from his dad's lap as if he were sliding down a funfair spiral chute and walked lubberly towards the washroom to get ready for the school.

Driver Raju felt serenely happy when Bhagi started getting ready for the school without bargaining for any more *Laddus*.

Sneha followed Bhagi into the washroom.

Next thirty minutes when she would be giving bath to Bhagi, dressing him up, helping him savour his formal breakfast, she would be reciting *slokas* from *Bhagavad Gita.*

Bhagi was to declaim the *shlokas* daily along with his mom. He loved these *shlokas* because during the night time, Sneha would narrate him the associated stories of these *Shlokas* from the Hindu scriptures like the *Ramayana, the Bharatham and the Bhagavatham* riddled with thrilling episodes of war, fights, challenges, sharp arrows, spears, chariots and horse chases and all the more about the stories of Lord Krishna whose childhood was peppered with charmingly childlike pranks.

Bhagi loved Krishna savouring ghee and butter.

He listened with undivided attention to the stories of Krishna who fought with demons at a young age.

Bhagi cherished the childhood, adventures and mischiefs of Krishna.

He fan-followed young Krishna. Krishna when he was a child never chanced to attend a school nor convent nor wrote examinations nor carried a school bag, nor travelled in a school bus nor had homework and never carried a progress card. Bhagi fancied and loved Krishna's infancy.

Whenever Bhagi posed the question to his dad how it became possible for Krishna to lead childhood without being accompanied by a school time-table or a school bag or a school bus, Daulat pinched the cheeks of his son gently and admired, "Smart fellow! You're growing fast! You're asking tough questions! High time you joined me in the business."

Chapter 2

FRIENDSHIP OF DANIEL AND RAJU

'Crime begets thrill and money; thrill and money are honey; crime exacts delineated precise execution.'

Twenty-eight-year-old Daniel was listening to a popular movie dialogue on FM Mirchi radio.

He looked at the closed window and the binoculars lying on the table. He sat relaxedly in a revolving arm chair placed across the table near the window. He had gauged his two-bedroom apartment and its paraphernalia.

He had expensive Nikon binoculars.

He looked at the watch. Time was up for Bhagi to leave for school. Daniel opened the doors of the window.

He examined through the binoculars the parking area of Sahithi Complex from where Bhagi and driver Raju would be leaving to the school in the Merc Benz car any time now.

The aerial distance between Daniel's apartment and Sahithi Complex was approximately 2 km.

Daniel stayed on the fifth floor in a five storeyed apartment complex. The complex was recently constructed in a posh colony. Two months ago, he took the flat on rent.

There was a reason why he had specifically rented an apartment in a posh colony every time he had devised a kidnap plan.

The police and the family of the kidnap victim would normally search for the kidnapper in the slums and rat hole like shady areas. They might not entertain a by-default suspicion that the kidnapper might be staying in an upwardly posh apartment.

At the time of occupying the apartment, Daniel said to the owner that his family was staying in Warangal town and would move to Hyderabad soon. He did not disclose to the owner that he was a Christian. He hung a photo frame on the wall of himself and a woman said to be his wife.

The owner noticed the photo and declared, "Your wife is like Goddess Maha Lakshmi!"

Daniel did not know who that female in the photo was! He selected her photo from a Telugu magazine. He dovetailed his photo and hers into one frame and got it embossed.

To make the owner and neighbours believe, he logged in household articles like sofa, Television, kitchen utensils, gas stove, washing machine, two steel almirahs, book shelves, religious books, ingredients of a *Pooja* room and broomsticks etc.

He purposely went to the owner and to one more neighbour separately and requested them to spare him a *Tulasi* plant. Pious and erudite sections of the middle-class society would invariably keep a *Tulasi* plant in their backyards – the hallmark of sublime spirituality.

He introduced himself as a senior insurance agent so that the neighbours would be scared in general to visit and disturb him. Insurance agents were considered to be an excommunicated class in the society.

He announced his name as Rama Rao to the neighbours and the owner. He fixed a wooden name board outside the apartment "S Rama Rao- Insurance Agent."

He ensured no trace of Christianity was evident either on him or in the apartment.

He had epitomised Jesus in his heart.

He eschewed the act of performing the sign of cross which was the natural gesture of a Christian!

He placed a large cement flower pot at the entrance of the house. He placed a *Tulasi* plant in the pot. He painted the pot with sacred colours and drew auspicious logos like *Swastika*, *Om* etc.

The owner of the house visited a couple of times and was immensely pleased at the maintenance of the flat by Daniel.

The office bearers-the Secretary and the President- and the owner extravagantly applauded him for the respect he accorded to *Mother Tulasi*. They unanimously declared, "Your *Tulasi* pot is the best in our complex!" Daniel bent forward in deference to them.

He gifted *malas* with *Rudraksha* beads to the owner, the Secretary and the President. He readily lied that the beads were procured decades ago by his ancestors from a holy location far beyond Haridwar situated at the base of the Himalayas!

In fact, he purchased dozens of fake *Rudraksha* malas from a street side vendor at Koti junction!

Daniel was a professional kidnapper!

One kidnap a year! Kidnap was all about meticulous planning. It was to be a bloodless coup!

Often, more than the ransom amount, the amount of exhilaration that he gained while he was plotting the kidnap thrilled him more.

He spent a month in identifying a right profile, compiling facts about emotional bondage in the targeted family, wealth and the businesses of the family. The victim was to be a boy between the age group of 5 to 7 years. He avoided abducting girls for reasons he alone knew.

He ascertained whether the father of the kidnapped was a daredevil or a prudent man with a pinch of practical common sense.

If the father was inclined to take the support of the police and lawyers, he would reject the profile.

He, essentially, selected a father who was filthy wealthy and intensely doting on his son. In order to cherry-pick such a family, he would befriend a male servant or car driver and gather minute details about the family.

Daniel dissected through the binoculars. Raju was helping Bhagi get into the car.

"Right time to go!" Daniel mumbled. He rushed down to reach the school on his red coloured Chetak scooter.

Daniel already established an amiable association with Raju during the last three weeks.

He informed Raju he was working as a servant maid in an IAS officer's residence. He said his master had an eight-year-old boy and one of his duties was to drop the boy at the school.

He bluffed that the boy's family was staying in Lake View Apartments four kilometres away. He advised Raju that his name was Padmanabham! He shared a fake phone number with Raju. Raju dialled Daniel now and then and the call had never materialised. When queried by Raju, Daniel casually clarified that the phone had technical glitches.

As part of the recce, Daniel, daily, would arrive at the school before Raju and Bhagi reached and would wait for them.

*****

Daniel was waiting at the school. When he found Raju coming, driving the car, he waved to him and released an expansively cordial smile.

Raju parked the car at the school gate, Bhagi got out and ran to Daniel in anticipation of scooter rides.

"Again, you're late! Come early, and we can go for long rides in the city on the scooter," Daniel promised Bhagi.

Bhagi pleaded for a ride on the scooter and Daniel obliged. The school was connected with an approach road from the highway. It was a pleasant avenue and had two parallel rows of trees on either side.

They completed scooter rides and returned to where Raju was waiting.

Daniel gave a Cadburys chocolate to Bhagi. Bhagi was about to seize it when Raju interrupted, "No, no, you had enough sweets today!"

Bhagi snatched the chocolate from Daniel's hand and darted toward his classroom.

Raju and Daniel were together. Raju loved to indulge in gossip. This gossip session was crucial to Daniel.

Daniel suggested, "Raju, let's go to our usual spot and have a cup of Irani tea."

Ordinary souls could not deny the offer of a cup of tea. Raju too obliged.

It was Daniel who reached the Tea centre first on the scooter, ordered two cups of special tea, a plate of Osman biscuits and two hot samosas.

After parking the car securely, Raju joined Daniel.

Both stood around a stainless-steel table in the open space in front of the Tea stall.

"Padmabham! What's news?" Raju ushered in the conversation. He accessed an Osman biscuit and dipped half into the tea. The biscuit turned half wet and half dry. Raju clasped the dangling wet half into his mouth with an appealing finesse.

"I've a problem. You're a shrewd guy and can resolve it, I believe," Daniel praised Raju ingratiatingly.

Raju smiled. He was consummated by the taste of a mix of freshly brewed tea and Osman biscuit, intoxicated by the oodles of praise lavished by Daniel and was feeling blissful!

"Please look for a new job for me," Daniel requested Raju, "rather, under your master!"

"What happened to your job?" Raju wore a surprised look.

"Let me tell you the whole story; my brother got married recently," Daniel concocted a convenient story. "He's a teacher in a private school and is a disciplined guy. Marriages won't last long if one is disciplined. His marriage, too, did not last long.

"The bride's family filed a false harassment case against my brother. Police were about to arrest him. My master is an IAS officer. I requested him to speak to the police. I requested him to lend a few thousand rupees to fight the case in a court of law.

"He shouted at me and asked me not to expect such favours.

"When a tiny request could not be considered, why am I to enslave my valuable life to him for a pittance of salary. Please speak to your master. You said he is a big business guy. I'm sure he must be enjoying many contacts with the police."

Daniel finished and looked at Raju.

"Oh my god!! Daulat is a stingy fellow. He would be more tight-fisted when it comes to money and secondly, he hated dealing with the police and the lawyers," Raju poured out. "Some time ago, I gave a piece of advice to Daulat about his sister. His sister is a musician. Her name is Payal! She spent crores of rupees and learnt music in New York.

"Daulat heard her singing popular romantic movie songs where the hero would attempt to win the heart of the heroine. Daulat worried that his sister spent crores of rupees to sing such impractical songs.

"I too agree with Daulat. In fact, there is no need for the hero to make an attempt to win the heart of the heroine who struggled to make it big in a heartless tinsel world! She already lost her heart in the process!

"Nevertheless, in the movies, the heroine would be shown, she had a heart. Padmanabham! Have you noticed the irony? The assignment for the heroine was to repeatedly lose her fictitious heart. The eighteen-year-old ravishingly beautiful heroin would effortlessly lose her heart quite often to heroes who were thrice her age. She knew it was why she was called an 'actress'!

"Often, I cracked jokes to my friends when I witnessed such acts in a movie. I said the heroine had not fallen for the hero. She fell down in front of the hero unable to bear the hero's horrendous treatment of the guitar. The hero did not know how to hold a guitar. He would rest the guitar across his waist and would scrub the strings hard! It was similar to cleansing the utensils at home by the maid!! Ha! Ha!"

Daniel burst with pretentious laughter. He willingly fell on the floor and knowingly took the support of Raju to stand up.

Raju's face was lit up with a sense of achievement when he perceived his friend was enjoying his descriptive skills. He continued, "When and which young man would come and fall in front of Payal's feet one day, not clear to me!"

One more round of profuse chuckling went on between them.

Raju added, "Daulat is actually worried about Payal for another reason also. She had a boyfriend who is an Assistant Superintendent of Police. He had an aversion for the police and the lawyers.

"Daulat would have given you free advice to settle the marital harassment case of your brother out of the court without the intervention of the police and lawyers," Raju ended the speech.

Daniel called one of the servers at the restaurant and ordered "Two more cups of tea, please!"

It was time for Daniel to stitch the burgeoning friendship between them into a strong bond.

He said to Raju, "Oh! Is it so? I guess Daulat, in such a case, might have been an agitated person. How are you people managing with a master caught in such a turbulent mood?"

"You guessed right. Daulat is a taskmaster!!"

Daniel continued, "Bhagi must be having a horrible childhood with his dad being impulsive!!"

Daniel gazed into Raju's eyes. He was all ears and eyes eagerly looking at Raju. It was the moment of make or break of the plot of kidnap.

"You're mistaken. Bhagi is the cynosure of Daulat's life. He loves his son so much so the Fevicol company would be tempted to hire the father and the son for an ad if they happen to see their inseparable adhesiveness!!" Raju drew an analogy and started tittering like a pony horse.

Daniel was ready for the moment and spontaneously enacted a huge belly laughter and spilled tea all over the round table.

Raju looked at his wristwatch and said, "Oh! I need to rush. Daulat will be waiting for me. Bye for the day. "

Raju opened the purse to settle the Tea bill. Daniel begged in a friendly tone, "I'm happy I've got a friend like you. Let me have the honour to host a cup of tea to my friend!"

Raju tapped affectionately on Daniel's shoulder, hugged him and left.

*****

Meeting Raju and Bhagi at the school had become a routine affair for Daniel for the last three weeks.

Same routine!

Bhagi would be taken for scooter rides.

Daniel and Raju would go to the Irani chai centre.

Daniel would purposely raise a topic which enthused Raju to gossip.

He ensured the topic ended on a jovial note so that, topic after topic, their friendship bonded more than ever.

One day, Daniel triggered the topic of 'wife vs husband'.

Raju said laughingly, "Husband is not an equal force and cannot reckon with a wife. Ideally, the debate is to be wife vs her mother-in-law. Both are equal forces, I believe..... Ha, Ha, Ha!"

Daniel erupted into laughter. "What an apt analysis! You're amazing," he continued, "and who is the equal force to a husband, according to you? You alone can determine it!" and chuckled.

"Husband vs who? Ahhh! Ummm! I feel it was to be husbands at home vs male bosses at office! Both don't use their brains but they possess a lot of power at their disposal!" Raju replied and kept giggling.

Daniel had not liked the crude analogy! But he opted to fall all over the place cackling with merriment. Raju tumbled to a corner with irresistible joy.

*****

Daniel stood alone at the Irani tea stall. Raju left for the day.

Daniel was gratified at the progress of the kidnap project. 'All the characters were falling in place!' he apprised.

He reviewed:

'*Daulat Ram was a wealthy man; a doting father; a discreet man who opts for settlement of disputes without the intervention of the police.*

Bhagi was a sweet six-year-old kid and was the darling of the family! And he began to like me and my scooter rides!'

The family was a perfect target segment for an abduction.'

Daniel planned, soon, he had to go to the supermarket to purchase sticker sheets, one rope to tie Bhagi in case of need; one roll of plaster to seal the mouth of Bhagi if required; and strips of sleeping pills and sedatives! Several goodies, toys, and confectionery to be bought!

Chapter 3

DAULAT WAS IMPATIENT TO RECLAIM TAPASWI HOME SITE

Daulat was reading to himself the maxim inscribed in the wooden photo frame fixed on the wall in the living room.

Destiny is unalterable; Time is immutable; One is a pendulum between the two.

He considered he was that pendulum. He wrapped himself in self-pity.

He believed he was alone working hard to get Rama Sastry vacated from the Jubilee Hills plot. None else in the family seemed to be thinking about it except his mother.

His mother, Vasundhara, of course, supported her son in his strategy to get Rama Sastry and the orphan boys thrown out of the plot.

He looked at himself. He was clad in a normal T-shirt and a blue jean trouser. A two-fold gold chain was visible around the neck and a gold bracelet was dangling on the left forehand.

Sneha offered a cup of coffee to Daulat.

He negated the offer and impatiently asked, "Is Payal sleeping yet? The time is 9.30. I want her to join the meeting with that nutty spongy old man. It's our family property. Payal should know the value of the property and the urgent need to get the old man and the boys evacuated from our land. It has been more than one month since I have been chasing Sastry. We, as a family, have to employ pressure on the old man and force him to leave the plot."

"Payal is sleeping yet, I believe. Shall I wake her up?" Sneha enquired.

She was aware Payal was awake and she already texted her. *"He wants you to join him during his visit to Tapaswi Home. Please get ready soon."*

Payal replied, *"Dad had donated the land to the orphanage more than a decade ago. I feel we should not lay our hands on the land. Anyway, I shall join Bhayya to Tapaswi Home now."*

*****

More than a decade ago, Janaki Ram, father of Daulat and Payal, gifted an acre of land to an old man, by name, Rama Sastry who was a philanthropist.

Rama Sastry was running an orphanage with the amount of provident fund and gratuity he received after his retirement. Sastry retired as a teacher and he had no family.

Fifteen kids were residing at the orphanage. Sastry was providing food and shelter with his own funds. It was a hand to mouth existence. The rented mini house he occupied could not accommodate fifteen boys. He was not able to afford higher rent and occupy a bigger accommodation.

At that moment, Janaki Ram had come into contact with Sastry at a community gathering. He admired Sastry's spartan way of life.

He came to know of Sastry's financial problems. He gifted an acre of land to Sastry and constructed an asbestos shed.

The orphanage was named 'Tapaswi Home'.

Vasundhara was not pleased to know that her husband gifted land to an orphanage. Janaki Ram managed to overrule his wife's objection and went ahead with the donation of the land to Sastry.

The land was located in a hilly area with no proper road, water and electricity connectivity. It was in a remote place and was a less developed pocket situated on the peripherals of Madhapur and Jubilee Hills.

It was an oral gift and the transaction was not registered. The original sale deed remained in the custody of Janaki Ram.

A few years later, due to old age health issues, Janaki Ram passed away.

As years passed, the city had grown remarkably. A four-lane road was laid abutting the area where Tapaswi Home was located.

A hill was cut through and state of the art roads were done. The land was now linked to the most prime areas in the city. It became a shortcut connecting Madhapur to Jubilee Hills. It turned out to be the most sought-after route for commuters.

Daulat happened to pass Tapaswi Home a couple of months ago. He was taken aback at the rapid urban development. He enquired about the property rates. One acre of land was now worth crores of rupees.

He shared this information with his wife and Payal.

Payal was first to react, "It was gifted by our dad. Because the gift was not registered, we should not reclaim it."

Daulat could not digest the generous statement of his sister.

He began to visit Tapaswi Home and incessantly harassed Sastry.

Sastry pleaded with Daulat to allow them to continue at the site. He appealed that he was promised donations from several good Samaritans of the city for construction of a pukka building to the orphanage. The news disheartened Daulat more. If the permissions and related documents from the revenue department were received for construction of a pukka building, it would become clumsier to reclaim the site later on.

So, often he visited Tapaswi Home and bullied Sastry.

Sastry promised he would not construct any building without Daulat's permission but neither was he showing any intent to vacate the site.

He was on the verge of getting a proper building constructed for Tapaswi Home.

At such an opportune time, if he shifted from the site and moved to some other remote place, he believed, it would be difficult for him to regenerate the goodwill he built for long. He was growing old and turned 75. The orphan boys had grown up and were studying in the nearby social welfare schools.

It was burdensome to move to a new place!

"Life cannot be restarted from zero," Sastry told himself.

*****

Payal came into the living room, greeted Daulat and said, "Shall we go, *Bhayya*!!"

Daulat had not spoken a word but walked out of the flat with a deadpan face. He was bidding to bring a sense of grimness to the work at hand.

Both siblings went down to the car parking cellar where Raju was waiting. Daulat sat in the rear seat.

Payal moved to the front side of the car to the left of the driver's seat.

Daulat summoned, "Payal! Sit beside me. We have things to discuss before we reach."

She reluctantly came to the rear seat and sat by Daulat's side.

She readied herself for a series of sermons. It was a fifteen-minute drive from their house to Tapaswi Home.

Interestingly, Daulat maintained a grim posture, detained solemn temperament as he intended to be serious, impolite and harsh towards Sastry.

They reached Tapaswi Home.

Raju drove the car rashly into the site, up to the asbestos shed and applied sudden brakes just a few inches away from the shed.

His intent was to create thunderous noise and manufacture a cloud of dust. He was successful in his effort.

Sastry rushed out to see what was the deafening clamour.

Daulat had been pleased at Raju's ominous advances.

While stepping out of the car, he cautioned Payal, "Let's be stern with Sastry!"

Sastry saw Daulat and Payal. He greeted them with folded hands.

Payal stood behind Daulat and reciprocated to Sastry's greetings without being seen by Daulat.

Daulat did not respond to Sastry. He hooked the thumbs of both his hands into the front pockets of the Jeans trousers.

He looked at Raju and asked him in a hoarse voice, "Raju! When are the bulldozers reaching here?"

So far, Raju was not asked to look for any bulldozer. Nevertheless, he was equipped for the occasion. He cooked up a ready-made lie and said, "Mostly, this evening Sir!"

Sastry implored and held the hands and the feet of Daulat. Daulat fixed his tone to a belligerent scale and announced, "See man, it's up to you and your boys. Either you vacate or face the bulldozer. Don't test my patience. I'm a considerate person. I offered you that I would arrange an alternative piece of land in a village away from the city. You're not giving up. You're adamant. You kept an eye on the value of the property, I suspect."

Payal was immensely agitated by a sense of compassion toward Sastry and the boys.

She experienced a sense of déjà vu when the memory lane took her momentarily to the melancholic song she wrote and tuned. The song narrated the lives of the destitute and the poor.

Daulat continued to intimidate Sastry, "I suspect you're not running any orphanage either here. Where are the damn orphans? I've not seen a single fellow the last dozen times I've visited."

Sastry replied patiently, "The boys go to the school this hour daily, sir! A few of them go to work. They will return in the night. We have no interest in the property value. It was given to us by your father long ago. I request you to keep up the word of Janaki Ram. "

Daulat shook his head in disagreement and looked obdurate indicating no scope to discuss further. He screamed, "Raju, the shed should be dusted this evening. Let's go!"

Raju aggressively reversed the car, raising a veil of diesel smoke and dust.

He then got out of the car, opened the car's door for Daulat and stood like the most trustworthy servant of a monarch.

Daulat thumped the shoes against the ground to show how angry he was. He sat in the car and whacked the door.

In a moment, Payal went behind the car and hinted to Sastry not to worry. Before Daulat noticed, she came around and got into the rear seat. She sat beside Daulat. On the way back home, Daulat said to his sister, "Payal! I'm not happy with your friendship with Sankar. Police are not trustworthy!" Daulat's dislike for Sankar arose from another aspect also. During school days, Sankar was a student of Rama Sastry. He was supporting the cause of the orphans and Rama Sastry!

Payal retorted, "*Bhayya*! I'm adult enough to choose my friends!" Daulat squirmed in the seat impatiently.

Chapter 4

BHAGI BOUGHT IDLY

You set the house dry and clean; We wet the floor glow and shine- is a funny caption in a poster which had attracted Payal's attention at the dog breeding centre.

One endearing Pug puppy and an adorable toddler adorned that poster. The puppy and the boy were saying those words while a housewife was fuming with a wet mop in her hand. Steel utensils were strewn here and there with drops of water being sprinkled all over the floor. The pug and the toddler sported a hearty and mischievous laugh.

"A dog's universe is a different world altogether. Pet dogs are not a mere source of fun. They will change the way you look at things around." Mr. Ashok explained.

It was a dog breeder centre where Mr. Ashok, the owner, was showing the breeds to Sneha and Payal. The breeding centre was located in an independent house. There was enough open space for the puppies to play around. The parent dogs were chained in the kennels.

"What breed is the puppy in that poster?" Payal enquired Ashok.

Sneha and Bhagi sat on the sofa enjoying the sight of a litter of puppies surrounding them. The puppies were agog sniffing the feet of Sneha and Bhagi.

*****

It had been for more than one week now Sneha was pleading with Daulat to buy a puppy dog. Bhagi was spending hours in the neighbour's apartment. The sole attraction in the neighbour's flat was they adopted a chubby pet doggie recently. Bhagi fell in love with it. The puppy was as lazy as Bhagi was. It was a voracious eater. These two qualities were more than ample reasons for Bhagi to be drawn to the doggie.

Bhagi declared, "I want a doggie."

Sneha forwarded Bhagi's request to Daulat.

Daulat didn't heed seriously. One day, Sneha lost patience and said, "Bhagi is spending most of the time in our neighbour's home. You need to bring home a doggie to make our son stay at home."

Daulat knew his wife's love for pets. He stared at her and teasingly asked, "Is the doggie for you or Bhagi?"

Sneha gestured it was for their son!

Daulat assured, "If it were for Bhagi, we should get it fast."

Sneha had given a sharp glare to Daulat and in a tone of grumble said, "So, I don't matter to you. Do I?"

Daulat felt caught off balance.

No one was around. Sneha was preparing coffee for Daulat in the kitchen.

He gently grasped her soft hand and tenderly seized her into an endearing hug, and whispered in the ear "I'm your lifetime pet, dear."

She mildly pushed him aside. She passed the coffee mug, "Here's your coffee. We can romance later. First, you bring a doggie. Or I would go and buy a good one. Bhagi is playing round-the-clock with our neighbour's dog. He is fond of its tail.

"Or you grow a tail and play with your son. If you grow a tail, we don't require a doggie. You need not be my lifetime pet either," Sneha turned witty and chuckled.

Daulat giggled, "I cannot grow a tail. I will arrange a doggy tomorrow."

He contacted Raju and instructed him to drive Sneha and Bhagi to the dog breeding centre the next day.

*****

"What breed is that doggie in the poster?" Payal enquired Ashok for a second time.

"It's a Pug," Ashok replied, "and it's the best dog for domestication. It's a lovely, cool breed."

Bhagi cheered, "I too love a Pug. See its tail. Curled like *Jangri* sweet. Get it!!"

Ashok had brought Pug puppies of different ages and paraded them in front of Sneha and Bhagi.

The puppies had frisked and sniffed around the feet of Payal, Sneha and Bhagi.

The pups had glossy eyes with streaks of gold and yellow colour popping on the pupils. The lens of their eyes was gleaming and their faces were twinkling.

Sneha bent forward to fondle one of them. Bhagi held its tail. He drew it along the floor smoothly. He cackled.

Ashok cautioned," No! Don't hold the tail. Hold the doggie this way." He lifted the little Pug into his palm with a sense of affiliation. He released it into the hands of Bhagi.

When the Pug stared straight into the eyes of Bhagi, Bhagi's face flickered with joy, astonishment and excitement. He declared, "I want this!"

The deal was over.

Accessories like tiny neck ribbon tie, trimmer, feeding bowls, pet bathing shower, dog waterproof and scratch proof car seat covers, odour fresheners, poop bags, dog bone, canine food etc., were bought.

Payal settled the bill.

They were on their way home. Payal asked Sneha, "*Bhabi*, how about a cup of coffee on the necklace road?"

"Sure!!" Sneha responded. She anticipated that Payal might converse about her marriage!

Raju had an instant question, "Will this doggy be allowed inside the cafeteria?"

"I would carry it in my palms," Bhagi said. "Let us claim it's a toy. Look at it. It's like a real doll. It would be funny to trick the hotel staff."

Bhagi named the Pug "*Idly*."

Sneha, Payal and Bhagi along with *Idly* walked into a cafeteria.

After five minutes at the coffee table, Payal said to Sneha, "*Bhabi*! I would like to marry Sankar. He proposed to me. I guess you need to convince my mom and Daulat!"

"Well," Sneha replied, "it's quite a task to persuade your brother. The hurdle is that Sankar is a police officer and besides he is supportive of Rama Sastry! Daulat's animosity for Sankar and Rama Sastry is well known. For him, all the police are corrupt. Give me some time. I will surely do my best."

Payal thanked Sneha.

Daulat held a view that Payal should marry a boy from a wealthy family, from the same caste and see a new set of properties and businesses be annexed to the existing wealth.

A marriage was to multiply the net worth of both the families, Daulat believed.

*****

Bhagi ordered Magnum Double Hot Chocolate ice cream at the cafeteria. It was his favourite delicacy.

Sneha and Payal were enjoying coffee!

Idly, meanwhile, slipped from Bhagi's grip. It began hopping around. Kids at the restaurant shouted, "Doggy! Doggy!"

The hotel staff rushed in. Bhagi told them it was a doll.

One waiter countered, "But it's moving!"

"It is a battery-operated doggy!" Bhagi clarified and he naughtily looked at Payal and twinkled his left eye!

Idly happened to see a wooden chair. The manifestation of the leg of a wooden chair looking like a long pole spurred it to exercise its fundamental right. It lifted its rear leg, balanced itself cutely on its three legs and sprinkled a few drops of pee!

Bhagi was aware a battery-operated toy puppy would be able to perform every act except what *Idly* had accomplished then. The hotel staff turned jumpy!

Bhagi grasped the intent of the staff to catch *Idly*. He pounced on it, seized it in his hands, ran out of the cafeteria and rushed towards their car. The hotel staff and the kids in the cafeteria roared with laughter. Payal and Sneha had a wholesome laugh.

Chapter 5

THE BIRTH OF A KIDNAPPER IN THE TWIN CITIES

"The sea horizon is an illusion. You, as a fisherman, have chased the illusion for twenty years. You've decided to move on to Hyderabad. Life in a big city is a different kind of illusion. You will be chased in a city. Take Care. God bless you!!" the church pastor blessed Johnson.

The church was located near the beach in Kakinada town, East Godavari District, Andhra Pradesh.

Johnson, aged 40 years, prostrated in front of the pastor, took his blessings. For one last time, he had bowed before Lord Jesus in the church.

Daniel, a 13-year-old boy, son of Johnson was looking at the pastor and his father alternately having no clue as to why his father decided to leave Kakinada town.

Both father and son left the church. They walked towards the beach, sat on the sand observing the azure vastness and vacuum ahead of them.

Johnson was a sea fisherman working for a fish trawler owner. He was part of the trawler crew trained in catching the sea fish, crabs, prawn and similar crustacean species under the sea.

Each trip lasted one month on the high seas.

Of late, a steep fall in the size of the catch due to various reasons including the change in the global environment was witnessed.

Domestic trawlers in India were not able to procure large catches along the East coast.

Gradually, the number of trawlers went down resulting in many trawler fishermen losing their jobs. Johnson was one among them.

His cousin, in Hyderabad, was working in a cinema theatre as a sweeper. He influenced Johnson to move to Hyderabad. There was a vacancy in the theatre for a watchman post.

Johnson decided to leave Kakinada forever along with Daniel. His wife passed away long ago.

He never realised that, after a decade, his move to shift to Hyderabad would give birth to a well skilled abductor in the twin cities in the form of Daniel.

Johnson was at the cinema theatre throughout day and night.

Daniel enjoyed unbridled freedom. No one tracked what he was doing. He was admitted to a nearby government school. He barely attended school.

Privacy and freedom when abused would cultivate vices.

Daniel learnt playing cards at a young age, indulged in betting, casual theft, smoking, lying and gambling.

He learnt street-smart shrewdness to readily concoct stories in order to walk out of tricky situations.

When his father was spending most of the time in the theatre as a watchman, Daniel moved around the city like a vagabond. He learnt to sell movie tickets in black market.

He grew strong and lanky.

He snatched dozens of gold chains off the necks of women.

He graduated from stealing bikes to stealing cars. He studied the insidious wiles played by the police to catch the fraudsters and kept his plan one notch above the strategies of the police. The more he travelled into the world of crime, the more he learnt the depth of deceit. He had fun at being a criminal.

A crime was to be executed without a stain of blood was his motto.

*****

One day, he was passing by a Maruthi car dealer showroom in the city of Hyderabad. The dealer showroom had a service station in the backyard.

Mechanics were attending to the clients who brought their cars for routine servicing.

A long queue of the car owners waiting for their turn to deliver the car for servicing was evident. Cars were lined up to one kilometre along the roadside.

Daniel spotted an opportunity.

He noticed the colour of the mechanics' uniform. He observed the logo on their uniforms.

He bought similar coloured cloth, and stitched similar uniforms. He affixed a similar logo. He soiled the newly stitched uniform with oil and grease.

On a Sunday morning, he went to the showroom area in the mechanic uniform.

He walked straight up to the last car in the queue which was far away from the showroom.

He held one clip pad with a yellow colour service sheet. He donned a mechanic's cap. He was looking flawlessly like a mechanic belonging to the dealer's showroom.

He scribbled the complaints described by the car owner on a fake service sheet.

He said to the owner that he would do a test drive to check the condition of the vehicle. The owner passed the keys of the car to Daniel.

The clients in the queue ahead of that car made a hue and cry when they apparently noticed a mechanic from the showroom bypassing them.

Daniel appeased them by informing more mechanics were joining in a couple of minutes to clear the queue at a fast pace.

Everyone around thanked him.

He wore the trademark mechanic cap, dark glasses on him. He sported a thick moustache to avoid being recognized.

He left for a test drive and never returned.

He sold the car to a gang of expert car robbers who dismantled the car within minutes.

Next day, he eagerly scrolled through the newspaper pages. It was reported a car was stolen through an act of impersonation by a fraudster.

He felt proud of his simple ingenuity.

*****

After a few years, Johnson passed away with illness.

Daniel stopped living with his father long ago. He came to know of his father's death. He went to attend the funeral.

Someone gave an envelope to Daniel addressed to him. He opened the envelope and saw a piece of paper with the handwriting of his dad.

"Dear Danny, please marry a Christian girl. Name the girl child your mother's name!! Your Dad- Johnson"

Tears rolled off his cheeks. He felt lost and remorseful.

He did not drink for a few days. He did not play rummy for a week. He had not visited his girl friends for a month. He did not pursue a theft or a trick for a brief period.

Such a feeling of abstinence born out of grief sustained for a few weeks with him. He resumed the old habits in no time.

Crime and sentiment did not go together for long!

Nevertheless, he preserved the piece of paper with words scribbled by his father in his leather money purse. The wish of his dad had unknowingly influenced Daniel to refrain from abducting girls!!

*****

Someone was jabbing Daniel from behind, "Hey man!! Move on or give way. I need to get down."

Daniel came into this world. He was in a crowded city bus going to Koti junction while nostalgic memories took him to the past.

No trace of the sea, the sky, the Kakinada beach, the church, the pastor, his dad nor his dad's coffin around!!

He got down the bus at the Koti junction and bought various goods from a supermarket. He decided the day was not far off before he kidnapped Bhagi.

Chapter 6

THE DUET OF PAYAL AND SANKAR

"Meditation for hours may fail to achieve trance! Chew a mouthful of chocolate. Next moment, feel a soulful trance!"

Payal read aloud to herself a caption displayed by a chocolate company on a hoarding on the roadside.

It was 7 p.m. She was driving to the Golkonda Resort.

'The company of an adorable young man will be the supreme form of trance' she felt excited.

It was a special day for her for two reasons.

She along with her two friends, Sandhya and Aditya uploaded the Unit's first song on YouTube. It was a three-month effort. The lyrics were written by Payal; sung by Payal; music composed by Aditya; video graphics, editing related work was done by Sandhya.

Payal named the album "Strings".

She wrote a lyric describing the vicissitudes of life!!

Three of them felt happy about the outcome of the project. They got it listed on all premier music channels.

Secondly, she dedicated the song to Sankar. She was now on her way to meet Sankar. It was his birthday!

*****

Payal parked the car in the Golkonda resort. From a distance, the resort appeared like a sparkling diamond.

She saw Sankar. He was at the lobby waiting for her.

She waved jubilantly and sprinted towards him. She took him in her arms, clutched him close to her and wished him a 'happy birthday'.

She saw at the spacious swanky lobby guests hugging one another. Some guests were checking in and some were checking out.

Hugs were aplenty; hugs of myriad varieties; a mechanically cold hug; an affectionately warm hug between a pair of intimate friends; a gentle hug; a bear hug; a romantic hug between a young couple; a father's embracing hug of a daughter; a husband's cuddling hug of the wife; a half-hearted business like hug of an employee with the boss in a bruised state of mind when the boss had not considered him for the promotion; an old man unable to hug an ungainly wife who went out of shape, squeezed her the way a ripen pulpy mango fruit was crushed by a child.

Sankar felt amorously cuddled in the soft and warm hug of Payal!

Payal and Sankar sat at a corner table specially allocated by the reception staff for the young couple.

Payal said, "Daulat was rude to me. He ordered me to stay away from you. I almost warned him not to intervene in my life. How long shall we deal in this manner?"

Sankar was keen to marry Payal.

He knew the approach of Daulat. He knew how much stress his master Rama Sastry was undergoing at the hands of Daulat. He was keen to support the orphanage.

"Let us not oblige your brother. He cannot prevent us from tying the knot. He's bothering us as well as Rama Sastry. Your dad had donated the property to Sastry more than a decade ago. It's unfair to claim back. Leave both the matters to me," Sankar assured Payal.

"Hey Payal," he continued, "I want you to meet Mr Noel. He's an orphan and prodigy in music, just 13 years old. He plays guitar and sings melodiously as well. I got him admitted to Tapaswi Home this week."

"A prodigy in music! Oh my god! Sure, we shall meet him tomorrow!" Payal was excited.

Sankar apprised Payal of his respect for Rama Sastry. He said he was groomed by Sastry when he was a student. He recalled that Sastry encouraged him to pursue a career in the police department.

Payal listened to him intently.

Chapter 7

SASTRY, NOEL, TAPASWI HOME

It was 6 a.m. Rama Sastry had just woken up and sat on an old half-broken wooden cot.

"The Universe is an orphanage; The Almighty is the caretaker" he told himself.

He was in a pensive mood. He opened the money purse and surfed the folders. Two one-hundred-rupee notes were seen. He had little balance in the Bank account.

He recollected how with a few lakhs of rupees of retirement funds more than a decade ago he started an orphanage.

His wife died of cancer. He had no children. He retired from a private school. He was to receive the provident fund from the Employee Provident Fund Department.

He shuttled to the Provident Fund office quite a number of times. A mediator asked him for a bribe of Rs.25000. He declined to offer a bribe.

He made repeated visits to the Provident Fund office hoping a sincere officer would, one day, settle the amount without a bribe or the intervention of a broker.

He was returning home one afternoon in the sweltering sun. Unexpectedly, he collapsed on the footpath and suffered a stroke. He remained on the footpath like an orphan for a long time till a passer-by admitted him in a hospital.

When he recovered, an idea had incubated in Sastry to start a home for the orphans and serve the needy for the rest of his life. He rented a tiny house and gave shelter to a few poor orphans.

Later, he received an open plot located in a remote area as a gift from Janaki Ram. A shed was constructed by Janaki Ram with cement asbestos sheets. He had been staying at the site with the boys for more than a decade now.

The orphanage was named 'Tapaswi Home'.

Rama Sastry was keen to construct a decent home for the orphanage. A few kind-hearted people had come forward to help him. The corpus amount was ready. He was looking for an auspicious date to start the work.

In the meantime, Daulat started chasing, pressuring him to vacate the plot.

*****

The sun was rising as usually unmindful of anyone's moods or temperaments.

Rama Sastry looked at the boys who were sleeping on the floor. Fifteen boys of different ages from ten to fifteen stayed in the orphanage. They were sleeping side by side.

The blankets they covered were not theirs. The clothes they wore were not theirs. The pillow-looking-like dirty stuff under their heads was not theirs.

It was a long rectangular shaped shed secured by four walls. It was covered with asbestos sheets. Two doors were there.

One at the entrance and one at the exit. Which end was the entrance and which end was the exit depends on the side from where one has entered into it.

There were no windows. Thc inmates kept both the doors open to ventilate the shed with proper light and air. In one corner of the shed, there was a rusted gas stove. It was not theirs.

Every piece of asset was gifted by one donor or the other. There were two rickety wooden wardrobes wherein the boys had kept the school text books and clothes.

The boys were yet to wear a dress on their body fitting their size. Oversized, shrunken, withered, worn, torn and faded clothes filled the wrecked wardrobes.

A broken mirror was hanging on the wall.

An old colour TV decked the table. Its picture tube had outlived its life.

Rama Sastry looked at the corner.

He smiled contentedly when he looked at a guitar kept in the corner. He turned his glance towards Noel. Noel joined Tapaswi Home a week ago.

Noel was part of a local orchestra which performed movie songs. The orchestra team gave background scores for street dramas during prominent festival seasons.

Noel sang as well as played the guitar. He was popular for his exceptional music rendition.

On *Maha Siva Ratri* days, every year, crowds thronged him. They danced around him when he had sung *'Jataata Veega Lajjala Pravaaha Paavithasthale' Shiva Thandava Sthotram* said to have been originally sung by Lord Ravana.

The guitar's high beat fusion emanating from the hands of Noel at the time of singing the Sthothram resonated the area with the pulsating dance fervour akin to Lord Shiva.

Noel worshipped SPB. He could sing thousands of hit songs of the celebrated singer!

No one worried about his Christian name. For the Hindu Utsav Committee members, his name was "Natraj'. They believed he was a gift of Lord Shiva.

Noel did not know who named him Noel!!

Local leaders organised celebrations on important festivals like Vinayaka Chaviti, Sri Rama Navami, Bonalu and similar festivals. Utsav Committees would collect donations in large sums. Noel would be busy during these festivals performing movie songs on the dais.

He earned a few hundred rupees during each festival season.

One music teacher happened to see Noel.

When he learnt Noel was an orphan, he approached ASP Sankar, requesting him to lend support to Noel. Sankar admitted him in the orphanage. Some patrons of the Tapaswi Home gifted a new guitar to Noel.

*****

Rama Sastry saw Govind moving on the floor in a bid to wake up.

He greeted, "Govind! Happy Birthday!!"

Govind thanked Sastry. All the boys greeted Govind.

Sastry said, "Boys! Freshen up. We shall pray; cut the birthday cake of Govind and he will distribute sweets!"

The boys got ready and they sat under a mango tree in a line.

Prayers were offered to the Almighty. Govind cut the birthday cake and distributed it among his friends. Sankar arranged the birthday cake the previous night.

Sastry proposed he would shoot a video pleading with Daulat to allow them to continue at the site.

The boys stood in three rows of five in each row and pleaded with Daulat, "*Sir!! We thank you and your family for providing shelter to us all these years. We beg you to allow us to continue here. We solicit your patronage."*

Sastry sent the video to Daulat on WhatsApp.

Daulat watched the video and his blood pressure shot up.

He contacted Raju and said furiously, "This evening, you meet Sastry. Threaten him. You take a bulldozer and pull down the shed. Get them to exit the site tonight itself."

Raju gleefully said, "Yes Sir."

Payal listened to the phone conversation between her brother and driver Raju. She informed Sankar!

*****

It was 5 p.m. Raju entered Tapaswi Home premises. He had the mandate from his master to be rude with Rama Sastry. He came to the Home along with a bulldozer and two thugs to wreck the Tapaswi Home asbestos shed.

Sastry was reading a spiritual book.

Raju got down the car, walked over to Rama Sastry and said peremptorily, "Safeguard your belongings before the shed is wrecked by a bulldozer now."

Sastry was taken aback at Raju's belligerence. He rose to his feet and peered at the two thugs and the bulldozer.

Absolute silence prevailed for a few moments.

Raju got angered and shouted, "You will not heed to oral requests, I know!"

He flounced toward Sastry and rashly lifted his right hand to smack him. Sastry shrank back.

"Stop," a scream akin to a lion's roar erupted.

Raju looked behind and found Sankar in a police uniform surging ahead. Payal was walking briskly behind him. Raju lowered his hand.

Sankar came, held Raju by his collar and shoved him to the floor. The bulldozer driver and the two thugs who accompanied Raju retreated after seeing a police officer at the location.

Payal tendered apologies to Sastry and she commanded Raju to leave.

Raju pitched in a querulous tone," Shall I inform your brother that you asked me to leave this place?"

Payal hollered, "Yes. You may inform him whatever you like."

Raju left grumbling and mumbling to himself.

"The situation should not lead to a fight between you and Daulat," a worried Sastry requested Payal. "We've anyway decided to leave the plot before the end of this month."

"Sir, I shall fight with Daulat till he gives up," Sankat assured, "and there is no need for you to vacate the plot. Please don't do that. I've come here today for a different reason. I want Payal to meet Noel."

Noel was introduced to Payal by Rama Sastry. She listened to his singing and playing guitar.

Before ushering to sing, Noel paid respects to a picture pasted on the guitar.

Payal peeped forward to see who it was. It was a picture of SP Bala Subramanyam (SPB)!

Noel tuned the guitar strings, placed it across his abdomen. He sang song after song, playing the guitar with such dexterity as to reflect the touch of vintage musicians.

His rendering was euphonious.

Payal was overwhelmed with joy. Sankar was pleased to see her wiping tears of delight off her eyes.

"Sir, we've started working on our second song," Payal requested Sastry, "and I want Noel to be part of the project. He will stay with me in our flat. Please permit."

Sastry's eyes gleamed at the wonderful opportunity that Noel got and he consented.

Sankar questioned her, "What's about your brother? He will not accept Noel to stay in his flat."

"It doesn't matter if he does not accept," Payal brushed aside. "I've an exclusive studio room in the flat and Noel will stay with me in my studio. I will manage it."

Noel was elated at the prospect of formally joining a professional music band and he thanked Payal.

Chapter 8

THE DAY WHEN TELANGANA GOVERNMENT ANNOUNCED PARTIAL LOCKDOWN IN THE STATE

22ND MARCH 2020

8.30 A.M.

Daniel relaxedly sat on the scooter waiting for Raju and Bhagi at the school gate. After some time, Raju and Bhagi too reached the school. Bhagi got down from the car and ran toward the scooter.

Daniel sat on the scooter with legs straddling on either side. Bhagi managed his way through the space between the legs of Daniel and he begged to take him for a ride. Daniel obliged.

Bhagi pressed the horn button and looked at Daniel.

Daniel extolled, "You're a fast learner. Yesterday I showed where the horn button is. Within a day, you learned how to use it. Amazing you're!!"

After a few rides, both returned to where Raju was waiting. Bhagi received the daily quota of chocolate and left to join his classmates. It was a Sunday and the boys had a special sports day!

"Bhagi and you're growing intimate. I'm happy for him," Raju said with an amiable smile. "It's good for him to have an uncle like you!"

Daniel grinned for the compliment.

Raju pulled out a paper packet from his trouser pocket. He offered it to Daniel, "Preserve this packet in your pocket. No virus would affect you."

"Virus? What virus?" Daniel ignorantly questioned while he unfolded the packet.

He found two pepper seeds, a piece of turmeric, a little coriander, a piece of camphor, pudina leaves and two cloves.

"Are you not following Coronavirus news?" Raju excitedly queried. "Since one week it has been all over the TV, WhatsApp and Facebook."

"Ya! Ya! I heard about it a little," Daniel reacted. "What is CoronaVirus?"

Raju sighed, inhaled slowly a deep breath and exhaled a ball of air at one go out of his lungs. He readied to deliver a gospel!

He figured out that his friend, Padmanabham (alias Daniel) had not much knowledge about Coronavirus and it was all the more thrilling for him to boast and make it grandiose.

Daniel was pretentiously all ears to Raju.

"Look at this video!" Raju showed it on his phone.

He opened WhatsApp, clicked on a video showing many humans falling like ninepins on the streets.

Daniel opened his mouth agape and said, "Who are they? Why are they falling? That's incredible!" He acted over-belief.

His mission was to impress Raju. He experienced an enormous kick to act superficial innocence.

Raju lectured, "'It's the effect of CoronaVirus. The rumour is that China programmed a virus to kill everyone except the Chinese. It seemed the virus was released all over the world by the Chinese through their agents.

Anti climax was when the virus failed to recognize the Chinese. It began killing them also along with the rest of the world."

Raju, then, showed a black thread hanging around his neck. A brass piece was tied to the thread. Lord Hanuman's picture was engraved on the brass piece.

"Jai! Hanuman! He will save us!" Raju declared.

"Has the virus spread all over the world already? What about our country?" Daniel queried. "I know Indians are pious. I guess the virus may be hesitant to step into India!" he added *masala* to whatever Raju was concocting.

Raju looked at the sky. Daniel too lifted his head.

Raju quizzed, "Have you observed any change in the sky?"

Daniel could not see a millimetre change in the topography of the sky.

He decided not to disappoint Raju. He responded, "Ya! Ya! The sky is not normal!"

"Examine the colour of the sky," Raju continued. "Usually it will be blue with random clouds around.

"Is it not appearing now in orange and yellow colour? And, surprisingly, not a speck of cloud in the sky! It is the first signal of the arrival of Corona. Corona is going to enter our country anytime. Maybe a couple of days later we too may fall like ninepins!" Raju wore a grim face.

Daniel assumed a look of daze on his face.

"Don't worry, Padmanabham. It's why I gave you the packet. Have you not listened to our political leaders who counselled us on the TV? They suggested carrying a packet consisting of two peppers, two cloves, a bit of turmeric, leaves of coriander, camphor and *Pudina*!! It would do the trick," Raju assured. "I've prepared a few packets, kept one for myself and distributed the balance to my close friends!"

Daniel tried to smell the ingredients in the packet.

Raju intercepted, "Don't smell. Those components are powerful and can do damage to your lungs if you directly take puffs. Instances of the blood oozing out of the nose, when anyone smelled this combination, are common.

I'm told they blend into a secretly divine formula when they are kept together like this in a packet."

Daniel folded the packet cautiously and secured it in the shirt pocket and thanked Raju. Raju felt relaxed.

Both walked to their usual meeting point-*Irani* chai café.

Daniel ordered two *Irani* chai. Raju lit a cigarette.

He inhaled tobacco smoke and exhaled huge rings of smoke into the air.

Daniel got amused at Raju's overconfidence and his inability to see harm from the cancer-prone tobacco smoke.

He was equally tickled at Raju's gullibility when he believed a packet of cloves, pepper seeds and coriander leaves, when kept in the pocket, would protect him from a deadly virus!

'Man is a paradoxical nonsense' Daniel recalled friend Vijay Bhaskar's words.

Gossip for the day was over, Raju said goodbye and left.

*****

Daniel stood reviewing the progress of the Mission Kidnap. He procured the tools, confectionaries and goodies. He extracted useful information through Raju about Bhagi's family.

He was preserving *utmost secrecy* about himself.

His friend Vijay Bhaskar, a senior to Daniel in the kidnap profession, long ago, counselled the importance of maintaining *secrecy*.

Bhaskar expounded not to marry when one was involved in the activity of crime.

Daniel asked him why? It was still a probation period for Daniel in the profession.

"As a criminal, you need to maintain secrecy," Bhaskar clarified, "and wife and secrecy do not go together!"

He added, "Stay away from having friends."

Daniel naively asked, "Are friends too a hindrance to maintain secrecy?"

"Yes."

"It's a universal belief that a friend is one who will keep a secret forever with himself, till his last breath! So, what's wrong in having a friend?" Daniel probed.

"A man can keep a secret till such time he does not drink a peg of alcohol."

"So, is it okay if I develop friendships with teetotallers?"

"Without vices like drinking and gambling, a friendship would not flourish between two persons!" Vijay Bhaskar concluded.

"What for, in such a case," Daniel confusedly asked, "we need to earn money?"

"You enjoy it. Travel the world. Do charity! I spend fifty percent of my money on charitable activities and the other half is for myself!

"Charity?! We, criminals?" Daniel was more surprised.

"Why not? When you questioned, 'We?', what do you mean? Are we not competent to do charity?" Bhaskar questioned. "Recall those days when you were a teenager! You stole a loaf of bread to satiate your hunger. Abject hunger made you a thief. You evolved from a street side thief to a kidnapper. You're smart. You're lucky also. Everyone may not be smart and lucky like you and me.

"Visit the slums, donate the money to the unlucky and the needy. Experience the satisfaction it gives!" Bhaskar reasoned.

Daniel was convinced.

He felt happy when he recalled his friend, Vijay Bhaskar. He phoned Bhaskar and chatted for a long time.

He thought the day of abduction of Bhagi was nearing. He set the date-23rd March 2020 i.e., the next day to execute his plan!

He left Irani chai centre. He drove more than ten kilometres away from his residential area to meet a scooter mechanic. He negotiated for an exchange of the existing red coloured scooter to buy a different coloured one. The mechanic showed a Chetak scooter which was yellow in colour. Daniel requested the mechanic to alter the size of the dashboard and guided him by how many inches the dashboard space was to be expanded. He wanted it to fit in five bundles of Rs.2000 currency denomination notes. The mechanic agreed to do the alterations to the dashboard.

He promised to keep the scooter ready for delivery the next day. Daniel paid an advance and returned home.

8.15 P.M.

Daniel felt deranged. He held the TV remote to smash it against the floor.

He ran amok all over the flat, walked over to the balcony and felt like jumping off.

He was shattered by a piece of news broadcast a while ago on the TV. He opened the cupboard frantically and took a Mcdowell brandy bottle.

He obtained a liquor glass, soda bottle and ice cubes. He hurled himself into the sofa; poured a large peg into the glass, added the ice cubes topped with soda water and gulped it at once.

He listened to the news again and again. His mind spun with despair.

What he listened to on the TV was what he had not anticipated in his wildest imagination.

At 8 p.m, the Telangana State government declared 'partial lock down' to mitigate the spread of Coronavirus. It circulated guidelines stating that restaurants, cinema halls, schools, marriage halls, and malls would be shut down from the next day itself.

Daniel angrily clenched his teeth, "DAMN CORONA."

The government's announcement imposing partial lockdown had virtually driven him loco.

The schools would be shut down from the next day. He would not be able to kidnap Bhagi!

He cursed the ill-luck. "Is my two month calculated effort a waste?"

He went out for a walk to evaluate.

He witnessed on the streets people scampering to the grocery shops. Long queues of men and women were witnessed in front of liquor shops and grocery shops.

He too stood in a queue at a nearby grocery shop and purchased adequate stocks for a month.

He returned to his flat and tried to sleep. He could not sleep when millions of ideas were rushing through his mind designing an alternative plan to kidnap.

9 P.M.

"Genius and the ordinary are separated by one quality – God gifted the genius with natural non-conformity which ordinary mortals call it rebellion."

It was a caption on the poster in the music studio room of Payal. Aditya liked reading it aloud.

Payal, Noel, Aditya, Sandhya gathered in Payal's music studio room. Bhagi sat in a corner. *Idly* was lying at the feet of Bhagi.

It was 9 p.m.

It was the second day of the proceedings of production of the second song.

Payal finished the lyrics. All applauded the content. *Idly* shook its tail in acceptance.

They had decided to shoot the video in places like the coal mines, the construction sites, the river dam projects and the road projects where the contract labour would be belabouring under testing conditions like the billowing dust, the polluted water, the unbearable heat, the unhealthy diet and the lack of basic sleeping amenities.

None of them was aware of the 'partial lockdown' announcement made by the government an hour ago. They would soon come to experience that lockdown was going to alter their lives substantially!

Chapter 9

DANIEL CAME ACROSS ALTERNATIVE PLAN TO KIDNAP

23RD MARCH 2020

8 A.M.

Daniel woke up late at 8 a.m.

He sprang out of the bed, grabbed the binoculars and hastened to the window.

He observed a group of workers converging in front of the entrance gate of Sahithi Complex.

The gates of Sahithi Complex were closed. The security staff wore masks.

Daniel guessed, the housemaids, the drivers etc., were not being allowed into the community for fear of the spread of virus infection.

Daniel could find Raju.

Raju was found arguing with a security staff member. After some time, he began to leave the place on a moped.

Daniel knew Raju's next halt would be at the Silver Tea Centre- an Irani tea stall one kilometre away from Sahithi Complex.

The tea stall might have been closed due to the lockdown. But, Raju would stop to light a cigarette, he guessed.

Daniel did not waste a moment. He rode towards the tea stall hoping he would be able to meet Raju. He predicted it right. Raju stood with a cigarette in his hand at the tea cafe. A mask was hanging underneath his jaw.

Raju saw Daniel, waved at him and screamed, "Hi! Padmanabham, I'm here!! Come, Come! Many things to discuss. I've dialled your number many times. It says 'such a number does not exist'? What's wrong with your phone!"

Daniel displayed a friendly smile. He darted over to Raju and said gasping, "Let me first compliment you. You anticipated it right. The virus landed in India now. Today, my master told me not to come for duty till they call me. I could not believe it. This is like an English movie script. I'm winding up here and going to my village tonight."

Daniel evaded Raju's question as to why the phone was not reachable. He left the issue unanswered.

Raju sighed deep and exclaimed, "Uhhh! Same here with me. I'm not allowed into the Sahithi Complex. The gates were closed as if Coronavirus were squatting outside the gate and could never cross the gate, if gates were kept closed!

"I too decided to go to my village. Shall we go together in a taxi? Which village do you live in?"

Daniel froze.

He had no idea which village name was safe to mention to Raju.

Daniel resorted to the same ruse he deployed whenever he was in a fix. He began to dissect his phone screen. He made Raju feel he was going through an important message on his phone.

Raju waited for a reply.

Daniel, with his focus still on his phone, questioned, "So, who will take Bhagi to school or tuition or out?"

"I'm not bothered. Enough is enough," Raju shrugged his shoulders and said, "We need to safeguard ourselves from Corona. Had I been allowed into the Sahithi Complex, the first duty today would be to visit a Dental hospital. Bhagi has had an acute toothache for a few days. He eats lots of sweets. His tooth decayed. The doctor prescribed treatment for the tooth decay. It requires two or three visits to the dental hospital. We need to wait at the hospital for hours, a tedious job. I'm scared to go to a hospital during these virus times. Visiting a hospital during the times of virus is nothing but spreading a red carpet for the death of oneself. This lockdown has come like a blessing to me! Thanks to the government!"

Daniel's eyes grew wide open.

He recognized, Bhagi was going to be taken out of Sahiti Complex for treatment. Treatment for anything could be postponed but for a toothache!

Like a supersonic computer, his brain was decoding the opportunities likely to arise now to abduct Bhagi from the dental hospital. Daniel had not enquired Raju, the name of the dental hospital. It was not prudent!

He looked at the watch, and dramatised it as if he remembered an important work.

"Oh! Raju! Your company is infectious. In your sweet company, I fail to take notice of time. I forgot to deliver medicine to my neighbour. He was critically ill. The mention of the hospital by you triggered my memory. See you soon. Let us catch up on WhatsApp. All the best," Daniel cooked up a story.

Before leaving, Daniel walked up to Raju to embrace him.

Raju stepped back, beamed a smile with a remark of wisdom on his face. He cautioned, "Social tension please!!"

Raju had mistaken 'social distance' as 'social tension'. He heard a CoronaVirus expert advising the TV audience to maintain six feet 'social tension'.

Daniel acknowledged, "I too should get used to the mask and the social tension fast."

He dashed towards the scooter.

Raju shouted, "Trust you secured the secret mix of packet in your pocket!"

Daniel already sat on the scooter and was about to change the gear. He questioned a little impatiently, "Which secret mix?" Before Raju replied, he promptly recalled the packet of two cloves, two peppers and other heavenly ingredients that Raju parcelled into a paper packet.

Daniel yelled," Ya! Ya! Very much. How can I forget? Thank you!" He left the scene in a jiffy.

Raju was hugely gratified with the compliments he received. He liked the friendship of Padmanabham (alias Daniel). He kept on waving his hand as a mark of 'bye-bye' till he lost sight of Daniel.

Daniel did not bother to look back. He rushed to his flat to track Bhagi's departure to the hospital.

He had not waited for the elevator but came up the stairs jumping three or four steps at once to save time. He was huffing and puffing when he got to the fifth floor. He barged into the flat, bolted from inside and hurried to the window.

When he watched through the binoculars, he found Payal walking towards the car along with Bhagi. He reached the flat at the nick of time.

He was familiar with the name of Payal through Raju. He saw her for the first time.

Bhagi was holding his cheeks in both hands to cope up with pain.

Payal took out her Skoda. Daniel examined the colour of the car and noted the vehicle number.

Payal and Bhagi left from Sahithi Complex.

Daniel inserted the SIM into the phone before he left the flat. He climbed down the stairs fast from the fifth floor. He hopped on his scooter and rode to the highway through the by-lanes.

He could not see the Skoda anywhere within eyesight. He searched on Google maps for names of dental hospitals nearby.

A few dental clinic names have popped up. He started moving in the direction of the nearest one.

When he was crossing lane after lane, he found the Skoda parked at a multi-speciality hospital.

Daniel stopped at a medical shop and bought a mask. All were crisscrossing with masks on their faces. The sight amused Daniel when he felt he could now wear a mask without any fear of being suspected as a criminal.

Civilians and criminals were masked alike!

He wore a mask, the signature cap on his head, sported dark glasses and sauntered into the corporate hospital. He was extremely careful about not coming face to face with Bhagi. If Bhagi happened to identify him in the presence of Payal, it would be curtains for his abduction plan. He walked quietly like a cat on its toe pads.

He noticed that the dental doctor was stationed on the second floor. He did not take the elevator but climbed the stairs.

From a distance, he saw Bhagi and Payal waiting in the chairs in the lobby.

He hid in a vantage position. After the treatment, Bhagi and Payl left the hospital.

Daniel walked over to the reception counter on the floor and politely asked the nurse on duty, "Ma'am, my master sent me to enquire about the next date of appointment. Could you please verify your record and confirm?"

The nurse asked, "What's the patient's number and name?"

Daniel noted Bhagi's patient registration number when it was displayed on the TV monitor. He advised the nurse the number and name of the patient.

She browsed the computer and answered, "You need to bring the patient tomorrow at 4 p.m."

Daniel thanked the nurse, came down to the cellar, observed the cellar area and left the hospital.

He felt delirious. A new opportunity surfaced.

It was easier to abduct a kid from a hospital premises rather than from a school, he considered.

He observed the colour and logos on the uniforms of the male nurse of that hospital.

'One more day to kidnap Bhagi' he felt relieved.

He called the scooter mechanic and informed he would come on 24th evening to exchange his existing scooter and take delivery of the yellow-coloured scooter.

Chapter 10

THE DAY WHEN BHAGI GOT KIDNAPPED

24TH MARCH 2020

2 P.M.

Daniel stood in front of the mirror and surveyed himself. He was impeccably looking like a male nurse. He covered his face with a mask and sported the trademark cap. He wore a similar white uniform the corporate hospital male nurse was wearing.

He maintained prototypes of several uniforms in the cupboard.

He had in his wardrobe collection- the standard uniforms of a police officer, a police constable, a traffic police inspector, a doctor, a nurse, a lawyer, the star hotel staff, the airport staff, the attire of a senior government officer, an army officer, a soldier, the courier boys, the pizza boys, the Swiggy employees etc. He possessed varieties of caps, spectacles, beards, wigs, moustaches, lathi sticks, duplicate pistols, fake barrel guns, stethoscopes etc.

At 4 p.m. Bhagi had an appointment with the dental doctor.

Daniel left the flat after seeing Payal and Bhagi leaving Sahithi Complex at 3.30 p.m.

At the hospital, he waited to execute the kidnap till the treatment for Bhagi was over. He perceived a kid with acute toothache would be an unbearable nuisance.

When Bhagi and Payal, after the treatment, were waiting at the elevator, Daniel emerged in front of them as a male nurse. He asked Payal, "Who is Bhagawat?"

Payal saw a male nurse of the hospital and she showed Bhagi. Bhagi was holding his cheek, his head drooped down and he was half asleep.

"Doctor asked me to bring the patient once again," Daniel said to Payal. "He suggested one more x-ray of the upper jaw. Please spare a minute." He held Bhagi's hand and began to walk towards the doctor's room.

Payal accompanied. Daniel politely said, "Ma'am, You wait in the lobby. Let us not crowd the place, please." Payal nodded obligingly and moved toward the lobby chairs.

Daniel began to leave the hospital via the staircase along with Bhagi.

When he was reaching the cellar, he removed the nurse's uniform. He wore a normal trouser and a regular shirt beneath the fake uniform.

When he detached the mask and the cap, Bhagi recognised him. He buoyantly screamed, "Hi Uncle! You! What a surprise? Are you taking me for a ride?"

Daniel said, "Ya! Ya! We will go for a ride." They reached the scooter in the cellar.

Bhagi exuberantly hopped on to the scooter. He imperiously stood on the scooter like emperor Alexander the Great. Daniel dumped the nurse's uniform into the scooter's dashboard. He sneaked out of the hospital along with Bhagi on the scooter.

He rode through the lanes and the by-lanes leaving a fragmented trail of his ride on the CCTV footage. Bhagi was drumming rhythmically on the speedometer of the scooter enjoying the ride.

Daniel entered into the lane where he had to exchange the scooter. The partial lockdown was in force in the state. The curfew would come into force from 7 p.m.

He exchanged the old scooter and received delivery of a yellow-coloured scooter. He checked the enlarged dashboard. He was pleased the dashboard would now accommodate five bundles of rs.2000 currency notes!

He left the mechanic garage.

Bhagi sat on the pillion. The painkilling sedatives given by the doctor worked on him. The chocolate bar given by Daniel melted in his mouth. Bhagi went into a trance and slept.

Daniel arrived at his flat along with Bhagi after circumventing the city lanes for two and half hours.

Bhagi drowsily got down the scooter. He remembered his aunt Payal and was about to enquire about her. His attention, meanwhile, was drawn to a street dog puppy of around six months old. The puppy was staring at him.

He sleepily slogged to the puppy, fondled it, and offered chocolate to it.

Daniel noticed Bhagi's affinity for a street puppy and said, "Bhagi, bring the puppy along with you! It's so cute!"

He wanted Bhagi to be as happy as he could be. Anything which would make him forget about his family for the next twenty four hours was welcome to him. Bhagi carried the puppy.

Daniel went to the lift when no one was around on the ground floor. He reached the flat without being noticed.

He decided to take a bath and freshen himself before he would call Daulat to inform about the kidnap of Bhagi.

6 P.M.

Daulat was relaxing on the balcony of his flat. Due to the partial lockdown, he was reaching home early.

Suddenly, Vasundhara came shouting, "Daulat, Sneha collapsed in the kitchen!"

Daulat dashed to the kitchen. Sneha was lying unconsciously on the floor.

Payal held Sneha's head on her lap. She was sprinkling cold water on Sneha's face in a bid to wake her up.

Daulat called for an ambulance.

Vasundhara briefed Daulat, "Payal has returned from the hospital just now and informed that Bhagi was missing! Sneha fainted soon."

Daulat got jolted, his voice trembling as he enquired Payal, "Where is my son?"

"At 3 p.m. Payal took Bhagi to the dental hospital," Vasundhara continued, "and she is claiming she lost Bhagi at the hospital."

The doorbell rang. A team of paramedics walked into the flat. They placed Sneha on a stretcher and carried her to the ambulance.

Payal followed them. She turned to Daulat and said, "*Bhayya*! I will call you in a minute and explain what happened. *Bhabi* is to be accompanied."

Daulat saw Payal's eyes tearful, swollen and red in colour. He realised an unfortunate incident happened in the family. He followed the ambulance in his car.

After admitting Sneha in the hospital, Daulat questioned Payal, "What has happened?"

Payal narrated in detail and confirmed someone snatched away Bhagi on a scooter from the dental hospital.

Daulat was crestfallen. He enquired in a weak tone, "Have you informed the police?"

She quipped a readymade lie, "No! I've not reported it to the police."

Daulat commanded, "Please note not to inform the Police about Bhagi's missing news! Don't give anything in writing to the hospital management without informing me!" It's an order from me!"

Payal merely said, "Okay. *Bhayya*!" She, however, did not inform him that she had already taken the support of her boyfriend-ASP Sankar.

She contacted Sankar immediately after she realised that Bhagi was taken away by someone. Sankar reached the hospital and both Sankar and Payal searched in and around the hospital before Payal reached home and informed about the incident of kidnapping with her members of the family.

7.15 P.M.

After some time, Daulat returned to his flat while Payal stayed at the hospital as an attendant to Sneha.

Daulat was in a dejected mood. He called upon his trusted staff and put them on duty to search for Bhagi! He was wondering whom to suspect? Was it Rama Sastry? He decided to do a search at Tapaswi Home!

He returned to his flat to inform his friends and neighbours and take their support searching for Bhagi.

A pall of gloom descended in his flat. *Idly* dismally coiled itself in a corner. Vasundhara sat grievously in front of God and was offering prayers.

Payal's studio room was half open.

Daulat saw Noel. His blood boiled.

In a fit of uncontrollable anger, he surged ahead, held Noel and dragged him out of the room.

"You get lost," he screamed. He held Noel by neck, pushed him out of the flat.

Noel begged Daulat to allow him to take his guitar.

Daulat was insanely angry. He returned to Payal's room and rashly lugged the guitar lying on the mattress of Noel.

He stomped back to the entrance door, threw the guitar on Noel's face and cursed, "Go on to the streets, you beggar!"

Noel managed to hold on to the guitar. He left Sahithi Complex in a disarray.

7.20 P.M.

Daulat received a WhatsApp call from an unknown number.

He answered, "Hello! Who's this?"

A male voice enquired, "Are you Daulat?"

"Yes. I'm."

"Hi, Daulat, give me a Whatsapp missed call when no one is around you. I've information about your son! Don't inform the police."

The call was disconnected.

Daulat reached a secluded place in his flat and gave a missed call. After a few seconds, he received a WhatsApp call from Daniel once again.

"Your son Bhagawat has been abducted. Arrange one crore tomorrow as ransom for the safe return of your son. If you take the support of the police and try to nab or pursue me, I will parcel you your son's dead body. Give me a missed call through WhatsApp when cash is ready. I will inform you where to meet to exchange your son."

Daulat trembled, "Please do not harm my son! I will arrange whatever you want!"

The call was cut.

Daulat wondered whether his son was kidnapped by someone for mere ransom? 'Was my son kidnapped by a professional kidnapper? Or was it perpetrated by any of my business adversaries or Rama Sastry?' he reflected. ``Had Rama Sastry planned it, the kidnapper would have demanded the Tapaswi Home plot and not one crore cash!" he analysed. He assumed it was better not to overthink and believed it was prudent for him to settle the ransom amount!

Daulat already made up his mind not to seek the help of the police. He had no worry about settling the ransom amount. One crore of money was an amount of pittance for him.

He contacted Dattatreya- Chairman of Saraswati Cooperative Bank.

Daulat had maintained all the bank accounts, fixed deposits running into crores with Saraswati Coop Bank for a long time since his father's time.

He contacted the Chairman and sought Rupees one crore cash to be arranged urgently. He categorically put an indent for Rs.2000 currency notes (that is what Daniel instructed). He said he would personally visit the Bank branch and would receive the cash.

Dattatreya called back Daulat after fifteen minutes. He said the cash would be ready by 10 a.m. the next day.

*****

Daulat informed Daniel that the cash would be ready by 10 a.m. the next day.

As proof of Bhagi in his possession, Daniel showed Bhagi to Daulat through WhatsApp video call. Daulat found Bhagi cheerful playing with a puppy.

Daulat gained more trust on the kidnapper after watching his son in the video! "Except for the cash, he demanded nothing!' Daulat felt he was on the right course to ensure the safe return of his son!

8 P.M.

The Prime Minister, Mr Narendra Modi, had appeared on the TV channels and announced 'complete lockdown' of the country effective from the midnight of 24th and 25th March 2020.

Daniel saw the news, got puzzled and went berserk. *'Will Daulat be able to arrange the cash tomorrow? Will it not be an issue to meet Daulat to exchange cash and Bhagi?'*

He contacted Daulat and enquired him whether he could yet arrange the cash after the imposition of complete lockdown in the country!

Daulat reassured that the Chairman of the Cooperative Bank was contacted by him once again and the Chairman sounded confident that the cash would be ready the next day at 10 a.m.

*****

9 P.M.

Noel stood despondently beside the railway track. He wandered aimlessly for more than two hours after he was thrown out by Daulat.

Initially, he thought he would go back to Tapaswi Home. He felt ashamed to show his face to his friends and Sastry.

He felt dejected when he was deprived of the opportunity to be part of the 'Strings' project.

He concluded that it was the end of the road for him.

He lumbered to the railway track with heavy feet, stood beside the track and readied to throw himself onto the track. A train was approaching fast and was a few furlongs away.

He glanced at the guitar. He stared at the photo of SPB which he pasted on the face of the guitar.

He reminisced about his performances and the raving reception he received from the crowds during the festivals. He sang hundreds of SPB songs on the dais which thrilled his fans. He recollected the little money that he earned during festivals.

An urge to display courage, a desire to flourish in the profession of singing had spawned in him.

The train went past him. It was around 10 p.m.

As he walked away from the railway track, with renewed vigour, he reached a church premises. The entrance gate of the church was open.

He walked up to the corridor.

He kept the guitar beside him and lay down on the floor in the open corridor. Warm summer breeze greeted him. He was clear in his head as to what he was going to do the next day. He slid into sleep in the proximity of Lord Jesus.

MIDNIGHT

Sankar dropped Payal at the Sahiti complex after hours of futile search for Bhagi at multiple locations in the city.

"Payal, you come to my police station by 8 a.m tomorrow," Sankar said. "We would examine CCTV footage."

Payal thanked him, "Good night, Sankar! I'm sure to be there!"

Payal crossed the entrance gate and went inside. Sankar waited beside his car outside the Sahiti Complex entrance gate till he lost sight of her!

*****

A disconsolate Daulat was waiting impatiently in the living room for Payal's arrival. Payal walked across the living room and didn't even care to look at Daulat. She entered her studio room and didn't find Noel there. She enquired with her mother and she was told by Vasundhara that Noel was shunted out by Daulat!

Payal confronted Daulat. An acrimonious fight erupted between the siblings. Vasundhara had intervened and forced them to retreat to their respective rooms.

Payal contacted Sankar and informed that Noel was sent out of the flat by her brother. Sankar's aversion for Daulat soared. Payal and Sankar decided that they would search for Bhagi as well as for Noel from the next day.

Sankar texted a crisp WhatsApp message to Rama Sastry: "*Sir! Noel is missing. I have deployed my staff to search for him. In case he reaches Tapaswi home, please advise me and Payal.*"

Chapter 11

THE DAY WHEN THE PLAN OF DAULAT AND DANIEL GOT DERAILED

25TH MARCH 2020

6.30 A.M.

Noel woke up the next morning when someone was prodding him with a stick in his rib cage, "Get up! Get up! No one should sleep here! Go away!"

Noel opened eyes and saw a sweeper with a broomstick.

He requested, "Sir! Please allow me to stay till the pastor comes. I will request him to take me as part of the church choir. I can sing and play guitar!"

The sweeper was dusting the closed doors and windows of the church.

"The church is closed due to the lockdown," replied the sweeper. "Pastor will not come. Please vacate the place."

Noel took the guitar. He walked out of the church premises and stood on the service road of the highway.

He looked around for a suitable place to pursue his vocation. He saw a department store across the highway.

He saw the sweeper finishing the sweeper job at the church and crossing the highway. The sweeper walked into the department store on the opposite side of the road.

After a few minutes, he emerged in a security guard uniform and took position at the entrance of the store.

It was 7 a.m.

Noel crossed the service road and walked over to him. He requested, "Sir! May I keep my guitar in the rack behind you for a brief time? I need to go to a public toilet."

"You can leave your guitar anywhere!" replied the security guard, "and if it's stolen, I'm not responsible!'

When there is no choice, a lotus flower trusts a muddy pool and blooms there! Faith is the law of Nature!

Noel too had no choice. He began to trust fellow humans!

He secured the guitar in the rack, scampered to the nearest public toilet, paid one rupee, and finished the morning rituals including bath. He scurried back to the department store.

There was none at the entrance of the store. The guitar was intact in the rack.

He turned to the church side, did a sign of the cross and thanked Lord Jesus. The security guard noticed Noel performing a sign of the cross.

He enquired Noel, "What's your name?"

"Noel."

"I'm Philips!" the security guard smiled. He offered a cup of tea and biscuits to Noel.

Noel thanked him. He saw customers waiting in long queues outside the department store. Due to the lockdown, customers had to maintain social distance which resulted in long queues.

Spread of Coronavirus and resultant lockdown had set in a pall of gloom among the general public.

Noel felt he had a chance to try his luck, entertain the customers and make a little money!

The management of the store had set up *Shamiyanas* to provide adequate shelter to the clients from the sweltering heat. The store was on the service road away from the highway. Plenty of space was evident.

Noel tuned the strings of the guitar, chose an SPB melody and began to hum.

9.45 A.M.

By 9.45 a.m. Dattatreya informed Daulat, the cash was ready. "Sir! You need not make a trip to our branch. After the announcement of the lockdown last night by the Central government, the police are on a rampage. It's like a curfew outside.

I will send the cash in the Bank's official cash van to your residence with adequate security. Bank's official vehicle will not be stopped by the police. You keep the cheque ready. The cash is arranged in Rs.2000 denomination, as requested by you. Please advise what else I can do! It's an honour for me to serve your family!"

Daulat thanked the Chairman.

He received the cash at his doorsteps at 10.30 a.m.

He, immediately, had updated Daniel.

10.30 A.M.

Daniel did a WhatsApp video call. Daulat showed five bundles of Rs.2000 currency notes. Daniel, in turn, showed Bhagi. Bhagi was immersed in enjoying the cartoon network on the TV.

Daulat sought Daniel to advise the meeting spot and the time to exchange cash!

Daniel warned it was not sensible to venture on to the streets along with one crore cash during the lockdown.

He said, situation on the streets was like a war zone. He informed Daulat that he would soon call and inform an alternative and safe way to exchange Bhagi and cash!

The city wore a deserted look. The police were on a rampage and except for youthful miscreants who were toying with the police on their trendy bikes, no one was venturing out.

Daniel was weighing other options.

He thought it was never so close and yet so far.

One crore of cash was shown to him on video call.

Five bundles of pink coloured Rs.2000 currency notes were flashing in front of his eyes. He was zealously impatient to hug the currency notes.

The challenge was where to exchange Bhagi for ransom money in a hostile lockdown scenario!

He saw from the balcony a person walking on the extreme side of the road.

That person was a rag picker.

The rag picker, oblivious of the lockdown, was walking on one side of the road collecting the refuse and the trash into a soiled gunny bag. It required a bit of effort to notice him while he was moving behind the garbage bins tugging plastic tins, bottles etc. He wore worn out clothes; the hair was dishevelled and dirty. A police van went past him. The police did not bother to halt the rag picker.

An idea flashed for Daniel.

He contacted Daulat and advised him to come to the spot in the form of a rag picker. The spot was an obscure narrow lane behind the GMC Mall.

He guided Daulat to arrange the cash in a worn out old gunny bag and cover the cash with trash around it.

He said they would meet at the electrical transformer in the narrow by-lane behind the GMC Mall exactly at 3 p.m.

He apprised that he would come in the uniform of a doctor along with Bhagi on his scooter.

Daulat hesitated. He felt it was weird to impersonate as a rag picker.

Daniel oriented Daulat step by step how precise he was to be while doing make-up as a rag picker.

He assured that no police would come near a rag picker. The deal could be finished off without being noticed by anyone, he guaranteed.

Daulat reluctantly agreed.

*****

The challenge for Daulat now was to look for shabby clothes and a torn gunny bag. "You should wear the dirtiest possible clothes," Daniel cautioned, "so that anyone should shudder to approach you."

Time was 10.45 a.m.

Daulat pursued the nook and corner of his luxury flat for worn out clothes and an old gunny bag but to no avail.

He was growing tense as to where he should go in pursuit of rag picker clothes?

One place where he was guaranteed of worn out clothes flashed across his mind.

11.15 A.M.

For decades, Daulat had not moved on the streets by foot.

All roads were blocked by the traffic police with makeshift blockades during the lockdown. Cars could not be driven without any hassle for five kilometres.

The police were patrolling intensely. They were wielding the lathi mercilessly on whoever they had come across.

Police vehicle sirens were reverberating the city.

One could see on the TV news channels scenes of the police being outrageously intolerant towards law breaking citizens since last night after the imposition of country wide 'complete lockdown' by the government.

Daulat decided to go by foot. He had to walk five kilometres to reach the destination. The streets were desolate.

He walked through a maze of narrow winding alleys among a mushroom of colonies to avoid being caught by the police.

He never imagined, one day, he would walk in the hot sun to fetch such worthless items like an old gunny bag and worn-out clothes. His eyes were wet with tears. The feet were aching.

His members of the family did not know that he stepped out of the flat at that odd hour. Sneha was in the hospital undergoing treatment. Payal was on the roads searching for Bhagi and Noel!

Vasundhara was at home and she was busy chanting hymns invoking the help of the Almighty!

Daulat reached his destination-Tapaswi Home! He was feeling thirsty.

Rama Sastry was seen resting under the mango tree on an old cot.

Sastry too saw Daulat and was surprised. He was more startled at the sight of Daulat coming by foot.

Daulat gestured for a glass of water.

Sastry hurriedly brought potable water in a soiled plastic tumbler.

The malodour of the plastic tumbler and the smell of stale water did not deter Daulat from gulping it at once and quenching his thirst!

Sastry was quick to update Daulat, "Sir! We're vacating the plot soon."

Daulat said the purpose of his visit was not to ascertain on which date they were vacating the plot. He explained why he came to Tapaswi Home!

"Why do you need a dirty trouser, sir?" Sastry enquired curiously. "A crumpled and soiled shirt? And of your size?"

Both walked inside the shed. Sastry opened a dilapidated cupboard. There was a heap of old clothes. He skimmed through the stack of garbage and segregated trousers and shirts of Daulat's size.

Daulat too chipped in. He himself combed through the pile of filthy collection.

He discovered one half-torn rugged trouser and one worn out shirt of his size.

He looked in all directions of the shed for a gunny bag. He found two old gunny bags in a corner. He took one of them.

He saw trash in a corner. He hand-picked handfuls of trash and puffed the trash into the gunny bag.

A stunned Sastry was staring at Daulat speechless.

Daulat started to leave. He did not bother to thank Sastry. He did not bother to answer Sastry's questions. He left Tapaswi Home with the prize of ragged clothes and a gunny bag. They were a treasure of gold to him at the moment.

1 P.M.

Payal had been at the police station since 8 a.m!

It had been five hours, Sankar and Payal were scrutinising the CCTV footage.

"The kidnapper was too smart a guy. He went criss-crossing through the lanes. He halted in one lane for a long time," Sankar explained Payal.

It was the lane where Daniel exchanged the red-coloured scooter with a mechanic.

"Let us go to that lane. Maybe he faced a mechanical problem with his scooter or something like!" Sankar guessed.

Both went by the police van.

They halted at a scooter garage in that lane.

The mechanic divulged that his client exchanged a red scooter with a yellow scooter. The red scooter was lying in the garage, he said.

Sankar inspected the red coloured scooter. A male nurse uniform was found in the dashboard. There was a badge with the name 'Lokeshwar' on the nurse's uniform. Sankar asked Payal to contact the hospital staff and enquire about the details of Lokeshwar!

The mechanic tugged out a piece of paper out of the roof of the garage, "Sir! This paper might help you. He gave this document as his address proof."

Sankar and Payal went searching for the address. They discovered it was a fake address proof document.

Sankar, in the meantime, received a phone call from Rama Sastry. Sastry briefed Sankar about Daulat's visit to Tapaswi Home, his collecting tattered clothes and a gunny bag. He inquired about the whereabouts of Noel. Sankar updated that an intense search for Noel was underway.

Sankar and Payal brainstormed the reason why Daulat collected old clothes and a gunny bag from Tapaswi Home.

Sankar got upset. "Payal! I'm not convinced about Daulat's approach! He's hiding critical information. He's not keen to take the support of the police. Soon, I'm sure, he will land himself and all of us in an awkward situation."

"You're right," Payal worried. "My brother is getting into trouble. He needs our support now more than ever, I guess!" *Blood is thicker than water*! She unknowingly soft pedalled for her brother.

"Daulat is to blame himself if anything goes wrong. He's too selfish," Sankar retorted in a repulsive tone. "He's not kind to Sastry. He's not kind to Noel. His sole interest is his property and his son! He will not trust the police. Who would be willing to assist such a self-centred man?"

"My worry is about Bhagi!" Payal clarified. "We may need to tolerate Daulat more than ever to rescue Bhagi safely!"

Sankar enquired, "How many servants are in your flat?"

Payal replied they hired one housemaid and a driver.

"We may need to interrogate them! Kidnaps in rich families take place with the connivance of housemaids or drivers." Sankar suggested.

"The housemaid lives in a slum in our backyard. If we visit her, she would divulge it to Daulat," Payal was apprehensive. "The car driver is not in town. He told me a couple of days ago, he would shift to his village. His name is Raju. He's not happy with Daulat as he did not settle his salary. I helped him to some extent!"

"Do you have his phone number?" Sankar questioned.

"Yes. Do you want to speak to him over the phone?"

Sankar suggested, "You do a video call to Raju. When he responds to the call, drag him into a casual chat. Don't inform anything about Bhagi's missing episode. Ask him to show his house. Inquire with him whether he has made any new friends in the city of late?"

Payal liked the idea.

She made a video call to Raju on WhatsApp. Raju answered the call before the second ring, "Good afternoon, ma'am!"

"Hi! Raju! How are you? Where're you? In the city or have you gone to your village?"

"I could not stay in the city! City is a hell. I moved to my village. It's a joy here," Raju responded cheerfully. "My children are enjoying fresh milk, thick curd and delicious ghee. Fresh air, fresh vegetables and pure water are available aplenty."

"Oh! Lovely! Raju, I've not known much about a village. Take me a tour of your house!"

"Ma'am, it's nice of you to remember me. Please wait. I will show you my place!"

It was a tiled roof house with two rooms. He first showed the two rooms of the house. He walked to the veranda and later went to the open area. There was a paddy field and Raju moved the camera in a circular way to display the greenery around.

"Superb! Superb! Really impressive! Raju! Do me a favour. For a temporary period, I'm looking for a car driver till you return. Can you suggest a name?"

"Uh! Umm!" Raju paused.

"Any of your friends will serve the purpose!" Payal hinted to him.

The mention of the word 'friend' triggered the name of Padmanabham in the mind of Raju.

"Yes! Yes! I know. His name is Padmanabham. He can help you. He's a bosom friend of mine. He and Bhagi too are intimate friends. He took Bhagi daily for scooter rides at the school. Shall I share his number? He's a driver in an IAS officer's house. He's looking for a new job. I will call him and ask him to meet you. I remember he told me he would also leave the city. Yesterday, I tried calling him a few times. His number is not reachable. Poor fellow, his phone had technical glitches! If he happens to be in the city, he's the right guy to take support." Raju excitedly revealed.

Payal glanced at Sankar. Sankar showed a thumbs up gesture. He was watching the video standing away from the camera lens.

Raju sent an SMS with the phone number of Padmanabham.

Sankar dialled the number. A system-generated response was heard, "*The number dialled by you is invalid. Please check the number.*"

Sankar said, "I guessed it right that the number would be an invalid number. Let's go to the school right away and inspect the CCTV footage."

Walking around the house, Raju went on elaborately describing the niceties and the satisfaction of a rustic rural life.

He did not realise Payal disconnected the call long ago.

He halted the expedition when he almost fell into an open well!

2.30 P.M.

Daulat surveyed himself in the mirror in his bedroom. He had returned to his flat from Tapaswi Home.

He put on shabby clothes. He wore a ragged half trouser and a wrinkled shirt that he obtained from Tapaswi Home. He left the hair unkempt.

He was looking impeccably like a rag-picker.

He ruefully smiled. *A billionaire in a ragman dress!!*

No one was at home except Vasundhara and *Idly*.

Vasundhara was dozing off in the Pooja room. *Idly* was asleep in the living room.

Sneha would be discharged from the hospital in the evening. Payal went outside in search of Bhagi and Noel.

Daulat rechecked the list of things he was to carry to the lane behind the GMC Mall. He took out the cash bundles from the locker, packed one crore cash into the old gunny bag, stuffed trash around the currency note bundles and he ensured the bag smelled foul.

He carried a tin of talcum powder and a fresh and chilled Bisleri water bottle. He carried a regular trouser and shirt.

He imagined Daniel would expeditiously flee away from the lane behind GMC mall after receiving the cash leaving Bhagi at the spot.

'The risk is Bhagi may not recognize me as I'm like a ragman. So, I need water to wash my face and a regular trouser and shirt to wear and appear normal and be identified by Bhagi.' he analysed.

*****

Daulat, *the rag-picker*, suspended the gunny bag with cash over his right shoulder and walked out of the flat. He wore a regular shirt and trouser over the ragged clothes. He scampered to the car, opened the door, eased into the car and started driving towards the designated spot.

The GMC Mall was less than one kilometre from the flat.

He doubted whether he should go by car up to the backside of the mall or by foot? He found it irksome to walk along the road in the form of a rag-picker.

He resolved he would go by his car up to the lane and would park the car a few metres away from the electrical transformer-the exact meeting point.

He reached the entrance of Sahithi Complex in the Benz car.

Before coming on to the highway, he examined the road in all directions. He was worried about barricades set up temporarily by the police to prevent the free movement of vehicles. No barricade in the immediate vicinity! None, except a few beggars and vagabonds loitering here and there, could be seen on the road.

'A rag-picker in a Merc Benz car is on the road!' he murmured to himself and felt self-pity!

He observed bikers riding crazily on the empty roads. The bikers were finding it fun to be chased by the police.

Daulat turned the car onto the highway. He changed the gear, pressed the accelerator of the Benz car and in seconds he was in the lane behind GMC Mall.

An electrical transformer was in that by-lane. It was where the kidnapper asked him to wait.

Daulat parked the car a few metres away from the transformer, removed the layer of trouser and shirt worn on top of worn-out clothes, poured talcum powder all over his hair, jerked the head left and right to help the powder fan wildly across his face.

He looked at his face in the rear-view mirror.

He was looking filthier than a standard rag-picker!

He glanced in all directions, having found none around, he got out of the car along with the gunny bag. He locked the car and reached the transformer.

His hands were quivering uncontrollably. His vision got obfuscated with utter chaos in the mind.

It was 2.58 p.m. Two minutes more for the scheduled time.

He noticed someone in the distance approaching on a scooter. He could see a boy standing in the front. It was Bhagi. His eyes jammed with tears of joy. He felt like raising his hand and waving to Bhagi.

He recalled the kidnapper's instructions.

One of the instructions of Daniel was not to wave hands at anyone. The second instruction was not to carry a phone.

Daulat dutifully left the phone in the car.

Menacing noise of sirens of the police vans could bc heard pouring out from the highway which was one lane away.

The scooter was now a few metres away. It entered the lane where Daulat was waiting. Daulat saw a young man in a doctor's white uniform with a stethoscope around his neck, a mask on his face and sun hat over his head!

Daulat's hands and legs were shivering hysterically. The distance might be fifty metres now between Daulat and the scooter. He saw Bhagi on the scooter.

At this moment, half a dozen youths zapped their bikes into the lane behind GMC Mall. A police jeep was chasing them. It was the lane where Daulat and Daniel were geared to exchange Bhagi and ransom money!

A woman constable and a male constable were brandishing lathi sticks trying to catch hold of the bikers who breached the lockdown rules.

A Sub-Inspector of Police was screaming at the bikers to stop. His voice was echoing in the area through the loudspeaker.

The mischievous bikers were riding fast to elude the police. Their triumphant attempt to escape from the police came to a sudden halt when a behemoth sized Greater Hyderabad Municipal Corporation's garbage tipper van entered the narrow lane from the opposite side. It halted in the middle of the lane. The giant van entered the lane to clear the overflowing garbage bin lying behind the Mall.

The bikers managed to sneak through the slender gap between GHMC tipper garbage van and the compound wall of the mall. The police jeep was not able to negotiate through the tapered space. The bikers escaped.

The Sub Inspector (SI), the two constables and the jeep driver got stranded. They got down the jeep.

The SI saw the sanitary workers on one side. He saw, on the other side, Daniel impersonated as a doctor with a typical doctor's white coat on him, a stethoscope around the neck. A six-year-old kid stood at the front space of the scooter.

Daniel could not help but reach the spot where the police jeep was stationed. He got stranded just behind the police jeep. Fear seized him.

The SI recalled eminent people praising, on the TV, the doctors, the nurses and the sanitary workers as frontline warriors rendering untiring service to the nation during the Coronavirus crisis.

He announced loudly in a voice studded with patriotism, "Let us salute these workers who are keeping the country clean in this hour of need. And this doctor! Oh Great soul indeed! Doctors are Gods!!"

He directed his colleagues to salute the sanitary workers and the doctor.

The jeep driver and the two constables stood in attention. They literally saluted the sanitary workers and the fake doctor Daniel.

Daniel wore a stiff smile.

He looked listlessly at Daulat-the fake rag-picker.

Daniel and Daulat were in a state of paralysis.

The SI observed the mask on Daniel's face. He admired Daniel for his civic sense of wearing a mask despite riding a scooter in a deserted lane. He saluted, gave way and bowed with respect.

The sight was akin to the guard of honour accorded to the Head of a State on the Republic Day.

Daniel thanked the police. He was anxious to leave the place. His eyes hinted to Daulat in a whisker of a second that they would not execute their plan in the presence of the police.

Bhagi, meanwhile, placed an indent with the SI to give him the police cap.

The inspector obliged. He put his police cap on Bhagi's head, saluted and said, "Would-be police officer!"

Bhagi ambitiously requested Daniel, "Let's have a selfie with the police!"

Daniel felt a thunderbolt beside him. He trembled when he realised how dangerous it was to pose for a selfie with the police, the kidnapped and the kidnapper in one frame. He fancied it would be a unique selfie in the galaxy of selfies.

He saw the police staff getting ready for a selfie.

Daniel urged the Inspector, "I need to hurry to the hospital! Many Corona patients are waiting. I will take leave! Thank you for your encouraging words!"

The SI obliged, took his police cap off Bhagi's head and moved aside with veneration.

The fake doctor fled the scene in a flash along with Bhagi.

Bhagi demanded, "Selfie! Selfie!"

When the scooter was going past the Benz car, he recognized their car. He shouted, "My car! My car!"

Daniel raced ahead at a furious pace.

When Daniel was fleeing, Daulat cried weakly in a faltering and choking voice, "Bhagi! Bhagi! Please come back! This Is your dad, please come back!"

Daulat contemplated whether he should divulge the truth to the police inspector right away, take his help to nab the fleeing kidnapper and save his son.

He feared the kidnapper might kill his son in an attempt to safeguard himself.

The lady constable awoke out of the patriotic fervour when she heard a whining sound behind her. She turned around to find an utterly nonsensical junk man so proximate to her.

She saw a ragman who stood like a billionaire.

Daulat was able to make up for himself as a rag- picker. But he did not know the unwritten rules of code of conduct to be followed by a rag-picker.

Daulat stood close behind the lady constable. He did not guess the level of irritation it could cause to her.

She got annoyed.

She yelled," Dirty fellow! What are you waiting for? I want you to disappear from my presence before I finish counting one, two, three!" She threateningly tapped the lathi on the road surface.

Daulat realised the mistake of having stood close to the lady constable. He began to walk away from the police and swiftly reached his car. He went near the car and was involuntarily about to place his hand on the car's door knob to unlock it. He instantly recognized the blunder.

The lady constable observed Daulat attempting to place his hand on the door knob of a luxury Merc Benz car!

Before Daulat took his hand off the knob, she threw the *lathi* in her hand ferociously like a spear towards Daulat and screamed, "You! rascal! Why are you meddling with a luxury car?"

The lathi banged Daulat's head sharply. He fell on the road feeling numbed and was half dead.

He lost control of the gunny bag he was tightly holding. The bag containing one crore cash slipped to one side.

The lady constable stomped toward Daulat shouting, "Before the *lathi* has even hit you, you fell down on the road! You, drama actor! Get up, rascal!"

She reached Daulat, aggressively grabbed the gunny bag and screeched, "Useless fellow! What for you are collecting trash? You messy creatures are responsible for the spread of the virus!" She tossed the bag into the hands of the sanitary worker standing on top of the garbage van.

She bent, collected the *lath*i lying next to Daulat and whipped on his backside. Daulat had now become fully unconscious.

She noticed the Bisleri bottle at Daulat's side. She thrashed Daulat again, 'Where have you stolen a new bottle, bastard!" She seized the bottle and flung it onto the garbage van.

The sanitary worker on the top of the van rammed the gunny bag containing one crore currency notes into a corner of the garbage van.

One sanitary worker stood near the garbage bin on the roadside. The second worker took position on the top of the garbage van.

The worker on the ground was collecting the garbage with his bare hands from the stinking bin.

He was throwing mounds of trash onto the worker on top of the van who was catching and arranging the refuse. They were working like robots with marked precision. Professional basketball players would have envied their passing skills!

The sanitary worker on the ground blew a whistle indicating they could leave that lane as he emptied the bin on the roadside.

The garbage van began to move on.

The police clapped for the sanitary workers once more. The mood of the nation was to admire and inspire the sanitary workers and the doctors!

The Corporation garbage van, had, daily, carried tons of sins of the city dwellers. In addition to the regular load of filth, it lumbered ahead with a crore of currency notes also on that day.

The sub inspector looked at Daulat who was lying unconsciously in the middle of the road and said to the lady constable, "Ignore the stupid junk fellow! Come over! We've a lot of work to do! Just now received an SOS message. It seems an incident of arson is happening at Kukatpally!" He confirmed on walkie-talkie to someone that they were reaching Kukatpally soon.

After a couple of seconds, the police jeep exited the lane.

Daulat was lying on the road under the blistering sun.

*****

4 P.M.

Daulat opened his eyes. He was badly bruised with *lathi* whippings.

He struggled to rise, walked over to the car and managed to get into the car.

He was in tears as he felt the insufferable physical pain and mental anguish of having missed Bhagi by a whisker.

He lost money. He lost his son. The police *lathi* whips were hurting.

He vaguely recalled a visual of the lady constable throwing the gunny bag on to the garbage tipper.

He drove the car in all directions searching for the tipper. He was not able to trace it.

He saw on his phone an incoming call from Daniel.

He guessed why Daniel was calling. Daniel might now suggest a different meeting point to meet and exchange cash.

But, there was no cash now.

Daulat had unambiguously decided what to do.

He contacted Dattatreya, the Chairman of Saraswati Cooperative Bank, and requested him to arrange for a crore of cash urgently. He proposed to cancel fixed deposits to ensure sufficient funds in his account, if required.

Dattatreya called back after five minutes and apprised that cash was not readily available at the branch.

'Sir, the Branch will be receiving cash remittance from the parent branch. Such an arrangement is allowed once a week only', he informed Daulat.

He clarified to Daulat that he would be able to arrange cash after three days.

Daulat was devastated. He was receiving incoming calls from Daniel incessantly.

He responded and explained in detail what happened after the departure of Daniel.

He said he lost money. Daniel had not believed. Daulat showed, on the video call, the lathi bruises he suffered.

Daniel saw lathi scars and bloody bruises on the body of Daulat and felt he might trust Daulat. He also reasoned that Daulat was trustworthy since he had not taken the support of the police inspector a while ago though he had a readymade opportunity to do so!

Daulat sought three days more time to arrange for the cash. He proposed he was ready to offer gold jewellery instead of cash.

Daniel denied the offer of gold. He said it was not feasible to verify the purity of the gold.

Daniel denied any other offer except cash and finally agreed to wait for three more days.

He worried it would be extremely tortuous to bear a boisterous Bhagi for another three days.

He constructed a strange premise that the lockdown had derailed the lives of not only the ordinary citizens but it disrupted the plan of each and every criminal on the planet.

'Fall in crime rate was not good for any economy,' he smiled at his eloquent logic.

5.30 P.M.

An exhausted Daulat reached his flat. He considered it as the grace of the Almighty that none had noticed him when he was coming up in the elevator to the fifth floor. He straightaway dashed into the washroom to freshen up. After refreshing himself, he went to the hospital to bring Sneha home.

6 P.M.

It had taken two hours for Payal and Sankar to finish the scrutiny of CCTV footage at the school.

They reached Bhagi's school at 3 p.m. The school was closed due to the lockdown. It took half an hour for Sankar to reach out to the Management, summon them to the school and access the CCTV visuals. The Principal of the school personally attended the school and supported ASP Sankar!

Upon perusal of the footage, Sankar and Payal discovered a man of less than thirty years was coming daily to the school on a scooter. He waited at the school gate well before Raju and Bhagi arrived.

Payal and Sankar realised he must be Padmanabham.

They noticed Padmanabham taking Bhagi for scooter rides every day and gifting him chocolates. Bhagi appeared cheerful in his presence.

Sankar concluded, "He's the kidnapper. He befriended Bhagi before he abducted him. He must be staying close to your flat. He was closely tracking the movements of Raju, you and your family for some time. It's the reason why he was able to reach the hospital soon after you took Bhagi for the dental treatment. He was within two- or three-kilometres radius of your house. He was coming on a red coloured Chetak scooter to the school. Yesterday, he exchanged the red scooter with a yellow one with the help of the mechanic that we met a while ago. Let us track a young man with a yellow chetak scooter in your area!"

Sankar commanded the school *admin* to share the copies of tapes of the footage with the police to get them enlarged in order to see the features of the kidnapper much more closely.

Sankar said to Payal, "Corona is a major hurdle to do a flat-to-flat search. I will ask my Sub-inspector to send one constable in mufti to support you.

"Next three days, I'm busy with review meetings with the DIG. You take the support of the constable and mark all locations which look suspicious. We need to choke the kidnapper.

"I'm sure Daulat is in touch with the kidnapper and is coming to know of the safety of Bhagi at regular intervals. So, as long as Daulat has not broken down, it's an indication that Bhagi is safe!"

Payal questioned inquisitively, "How're you so sure Daulat is in contact with the kidnapper?"

"When I reviewed the history of kidnap crimes in the rich families," Sankar answered, "I recalled that someone in the family was secretly in contact with the kidnapper. The kidnapper would select the most gullible one in the family to initiate a dialogue with him. In this case, it is Daulat. Who manages the bank accounts in your sweets business firm? Ask the accountant if any large withdrawal of cash took place in the last two days from the account of the firm or Daulat's account? If the reply is yes, it means Daulat readied the ransom amount."

Payal looked at Sankar appreciatively, "I will check with our accountant. Anyway, if Daulat's plan turns successful, Bhagi will safely return home. Is it not good news for us?"

"The secret arrangement between Daulat and the kidnapper might go topsy-turvy anytime," Sankar warned. "A nasty misunderstanding will inadvertently result in the death of the child or the parent or the kidnapper."

Payal sighed deeply trying to relieve herself from the amount of stress engulfed her at the moment.

Sankar asked, "Has the hospital staff informed who Lokeshwar is?"

"The hospital staff required me to lodge a formal complaint in order to divulge any kind of information. I've given a written complaint. They didn't accept it. They want the complaint to be given by the father of the missing boy! Daulat is not willing to lodge a formal complaint!" said Payal.

"Daulat has become a big obstacle in this case! I'm seriously upset with him. You permit me," Sankar affirmed, "and I will, at first, arrest Daulat!"

Payal remained calm!

*****

7 P.M.

When Payal stepped into the flat, the question shot by an impatient Daulat was, "Payal! Hope you have not contacted the police?"

Payal stated, "No! No! Not at all!"

"You're a liar!" Daulat roared.

She was puzzled.

Daulat's vocal cords burst into pieces when he hollered furiously, "The school principal called me and said you and your friend ASP Sankar were at the school and went through the CCTV footage!! She enquired me whether all is well at home. Why have you informed Sankar about Bhagi's kidnap! You leave my house! You don't deserve to stay with me! You want to see the death of Bhagi."

Payal was frozen with shock.

Sneha was discharged from the hospital and she was resting in the bedroom. She overheard the shouts of her husband. She came hurriedly to pacify Daulat. Daulat jostled her aside and thundered, "Payal has no place in my flat!"

Payal decided to leave. Vasundhara intervened and held her daughter.

Payal said in a calm voice, "*Maa*! I will be fine. I will return when everything is normal."

An antagonised Payal walked out of the flat.

She was about to enter the car, Sneha came running to the cellar and handed her a few pairs of clothes, guitar, laptop, phone charger etc. Payal thanked her and hugged her tight.

"Where will you go?" a tearful Sneha enquired.

"I will stay with Aditya. I will be in touch with you."

Payal drove out of Sahithi Complex in her Skoda. Aditya's house was a stone's throw away from Sahithi complex. She contacted Sankar and briefed him about the fight that happened a while ago between her and Daulat!

"How come you've a brother like Daulat? Both of you're South and North poles! Daulat is a heartless fellow!" whined a frustrated Sankar. "He kicked out Noel. We don't know where Noel is. The poor boy might be suffering without food and shelter.

"Today, he asked his own sister to leave the flat.

"He is a demon.

"He holds a unilateral viewpoint that the entire police department is corrupt.

"He will soon acknowledge that our department has honest and efficient officers. I will find Bhagi and Noel!"

Payal thanked Sankar.

9 P.M.

Noel was ecstatic.

He was enormously thrilled at the response he received from the customers at the department store.

In the morning, when he was looking around the store, he saw in a corner a half broken plastic chair. He tied the broken legs of the chair with ropes and made it user friendly.

He gently and amiably touched the soundboard of the guitar, tuned the guitar strings and sat on the plastic chair.

He closed his eyes and offered prayer to Jesus; he prayed to Lord Shiva; he paid respects to Rama Sastry, remembered the music teacher who helped him join in Tapaswi Home and thanked Payal-his new mentor.

He reverently touched the picture of SPB.

He went on humming for a few moments before he began to sing melody after melody while simultaneously playing the guitar.

Customers at the department store were mesmerised. They clapped rapturously.

Someone thanked the Manager of the store for arranging such a heart-warming musical treat and relieving them from the ordeal of spending distressful hours during the challenging times unleashed by Coronavirus.

The Manager replied it was not arranged by the store. He said the boy was an orphan.

At this news, the customers at the store felt boundless empathy toward Noel. They took heaps of selfies with him.

Videos were shot. The video clips were posted on WhatsApp, Facebook, Instagram and Twitter. Comments like "a prodigious music talent and an orphan" went viral.

Someone pushed a ten rupee note into Noel's shirt pocket. A few more followed. Later, everyone gave cash to him. His pockets were surfeit with cash.

One customer requested, "Can you play Hindi songs?"

Noel sang, '*Mera Jeevan Kora Kaagaj*!'

The place resonated with applause.

Philips arranged lunch for Noel and permitted him to take a nap in the afternoon in the church.

Noel returned at 4 pm to the store, resumed his performance and continued till 8 p.m.

At the end of the session, he collected a substantial amount of cash. He did not bother to count the money. He gave the money to Philips and requested to secure it with him.

The Manager of the store requested Noel to continue the show the next day.

That night, Philips allowed Noel to lie down and sleep comfortably on a long wooden bench inside the church.

Noel thought he would soon go to Tapaswi Home and share his little fortune with his friends and Rama Sastry.

Chapter 12

DANIEL'S TRAVAILS WITH BHAGI

26TH MARCH 2020

7 A.M

Daniel managed to sleep for a couple of hours last night. For more than three decades, he got used to an erratic sleep pattern.

The feature of uncertainty had been a part of his routine.

He was savouring coffee standing on the balcony.

He looked into his flat. Bhagi was in a deep sleep on the couch. Daniel perceived that sound sleep was an indication of the scale of the warmth Bhagi was feeling in his flat.

He never compromised on the arrangements that he provided to the kidnapped children. He believed the kids from affluent families could not be detained for long in messy conditions. Vijay Bhaskar, his friend, tutored him about this critical point.

He equipped the house with expensive sofas, smart TV, Air conditioners, cushioned beds, soft pillows, carpets, flashy mirrors, laptops, washing machines with driers, expensive refrigerators, perfumes, imported room fresheners and latest electronic gadgets like Spy Night vision goggles, Creative Starter kits etc.

The kidnapped and affluent kid was treated like a VIP guest.

He cultivated Himalayan size of forbearance to humour a six-year-old boy born with a silver spoon.

His experience taught him he should pamper the kid so much that the boy was not to remember the members of the family and friends during the period of hostage.

But lockdown had thrown a new set of challenges to Daniel.

Lockdown disrupted.

The first disruption was that no additional pair of clothes was there to offer to Bhagi. It was more than one day Bhagi was wearing the same pair of clothes.

He was habituated to changing branded shirts and knickers twice a day.

Last night, Bhagi complained his shirt was smelling of sweat. He wore an irritable face.

Daniel alerted himself, he felt he should urgently arrange one fresh shirt and a half trouser at Bhagi's disposal.

He looked around from the balcony. He saw a housemaid on the opposite side of his flat carrying two buckets full of clothes and walking towards the elevator.

He grasped she was going to the open terrace to spread the washed clothes across the plastic ropes.

He patiently waited till she returned with empty buckets, then, he came inside his flat, closed the balcony door and examined Bhagi. Bhagi was snoring.

He cautiously bent over Bhagi, measured with both hands the waist and the chest of Bhagi to feel his size.

He walked out of the flat, locked from outside and scurried to the top floor.

On the open terrace, he saw rows of wet clothes tied to the ropes. The hanging clothes appeared like under-trial criminals. The rising morning Sun was gearing up to roast them.

He detected various sizes of blouses, undergarments, shirts, trousers, half trousers, T shirts, gowns etc.

He noticed none of the dresses were normal in size. It made him believe the middle class of the country were doing well. Obesity seemed a norm.

Yet, he struggled to identify one half trouser and one T-shirt which might fit Bhagi's bulky carriage. Bhagi did not belong to the middle class and he was a tad more obese than the middle class boys!

He snatched one pair and returned to his flat. The clothes were wet and he placed them into the drier.

Bhagi was a voracious eater. He relished Masala omelettes, Maggie noodles of tomato flavour, stuffed Almond Methi parathas as his first choice followed by *Laddus* and Cadbury chocolates; lastly, a glass full of *lassi* would be swilled on top of such load to push it down the throat and into the gorge called 'the belly'.

Daniel trained himself in culinary arts. He joined formal cooking classes and became an expert chef especially of food which would be of liking to the kids. The shortest route to keep the kids cheerful was to serve them hot and delicious food of their fondness.

On that morning, Daniel readied stuffed Almond Methi parathas and masala omelette for Bhagi. Spoonfuls of cow ghee and Amul butter were spread on the parathas. Sweet *lassi* was done and kept in the refrigerator ready.

The whiff of masala omelette and parathas floated and touched the nostrils of Bhagi, he spontaneously woke up and cooed, "*Mom*!"

Daniel dashed to Bhagi. His immediate task was to keep Bhagi away from remembering his *mom*. He helped him brush his teeth. He abundantly celebrated Bhagi's skills at playing video games. He lavishly praised, "You played the games on the smart TV so brilliantly last night. You're a wonderful boy.....a genius!"

Bhagi felt gratified and beamed a pleasant grin.

He bathed and the ablutions were over. He loved the fragrance of the body soap and the foam and perfume generated by shampoo.

He was offered a new Bombay Dyeing bush towel to dry himself up. He used the towel and threw it into a corner. He stood naked anticipating a new set of dresses.

He expected a pair of Gini & Joni or United Colours of Benetton like branded T shirt and trousers which was what he would normally wear at home.

Daniel brought a pair of dried cotton discoloured shirts and trousers.

Bhagi put on an astonished face.

Daniel, unmindful of Bhagi's astonishment, tried to fit the dress on Bhagi. The shirt could venture up to his chest. Bhagi's head got stuck in the shirt, his hands went up through the sleeves pointing to the sky and Daniel applied more force to normalise the unusual posture. The shirt travelled down a few more inches and it rammed Bhagi's hands and neck into an un-manoeuvrable position.

Any kid would have panicked and cried for help.

Bhagi innocently enquired, "How do I eat omelette now?"

Daniel could not stop laughing. Bhagi too laughed. More laughter followed, flexing Bhagi's muscles to stretch more, helping the shirt and the trouser ease onto him.

Bhagi stretched his hands suggesting to Daniel to hoist him.

Daniel inhaled a deep breath, did an explosive movement in the thighs and shoulders and bent forward, the way a wrestler would squat before he lifted a heavy weight.

He took Bhagi on him and started ploughing himself out of the washroom like a weak buffalo pulling a heavy wooden plough across the paddy field.

Bhagi began to sing a jingle loudly and merrily.

Daniel was relieved to see Bhagi in a buoyant mood.

He did not waste much time. He placed a *teapoy* in front of the couch, garnished the omelette, the stuffed parathas in silver plates and a glass of lassi on the *teapoy*.

He dropped Bhagi on the couch and switched on Television.

Bhagi launched. Omelette and Parathas disappeared. *Lassi* evaporated.

*****

Daniel had one more exigent chore to attend. After breakfast, Bhagi would surely ask for a smart phone.

On the 24th evening, when Daniel was about to flee from the hospital cellar along with Bhagi, he asked his VIP guest, "Hi Bhagi! Where's your phone?"

He knew Bhagi had a smartphone. It was risky to allow him to possess a phone with him.

"It was with Payal aunty," Bhagi replied. "When I went into the doctor's room for treatment, I gave my phone to aunty. She kept it in her vanity bag! Shall we go back and take it?"

"No! Not required. I will buy you a new one!" Daniel promised.

"Will you buy me a new phone today? Now?" Bhagi questioned excitedly.

"Ya! I will buy it tomorrow evening!" Daniel reassured him.

He did not want to give a false promise to a kid. He learnt that it would be hazardous to lie to the kids.

Kids would remember with razor sharp memory, the dates promised by the elders to buy a gift for them.

If the elders failed to deliver the gift on the chosen date, hell would break loose in the house. It was the reason why Daniel preferred to be truthful.

"Will you come to my flat to take me shopping tomorrow?" Bhagi enquired.

Daniel disclosed, "You're going to stay with me today and tomorrow! I requested your dad and he obliged. I love you. I believe you too like my company!"

There was a moment of pause.

Bhagi snapped, "Do you have a smart TV to play games?"

"Yes! I have. I also have a laptop."

Bhagi complained, "But, my smart phone is not with me!"

"I promised I would buy a new one tomorrow!". Daniel reiterated.

He assumed such a necessity to buy a new phone the next evening should not arise because he was sure he would free Bhagi the next morning. But, he was not able to get rid of Bhagi. He was stuck with him for the next two days at least. It was nerve-wracking.

His worry had a reason. Bhagi began to ask Daniel his phone to make calls to his dad and mom. He was eager to tell his dad and mom how much he was enjoying Daniel's company. He knew their phone numbers by heart.

Daniel made sure he kept his phone away from Bhagi. Bhagi was constantly tracking to see where Daniel was hiding the phone.

Last night, when Daniel inattentively kept the phone on the desk, Bhagi snatched it and noiselessly sneaked into the washroom.

Daniel was busy making dinner. At the nick of time, he happened to see Bhagi going quietly into the washroom with a phone in his hand. Bhagi went inside and bolted the door.

Daniel recognised the danger. He was not sure whether minimum time lapsed or not which would ensure the phone got auto-locked. He screeched, "HI! Bhagi! You're a good boy! Come out please! Kids should not touch their elders' phones!"

"I will make just one call to my dad. I want to inform him how happy I'm here! I want to thank him." Bhagi replied.

Daniel overheard the cracking noise of the number keys pad of the phone. It meant that Bhagi started dialling on the phone.

Daniel screamed, "Take care! An ugly monstrous cockroach is in the corner below the washbasin."

The mention of cockroach scared so precisely, next moment, a bursting blast of Bhagi's body violently being knocked out of the washroom was witnessed by Daniel.

The jangling noise of a phone flying and hitting the floor was heard.

Daniel hassled towards his phone which crashed into a corner. He picked it up and at first went through the call history. The phone was intact. The call had not materialised. No outgoing call was evident.

Bhagi was gasping, lying on the floor!

Later, Daniel realised that had he stayed calm as ever and thought in a cool way, he could have simply disconnected the Wi-Fi connection to disable any calls going from the phone. He had no SIM in the phone anyway. 'Is fear an uncontrollable emotion?' he quizzed himself.

The consequence of the cockroach incident resulted in Bhagi not willing to go to the washroom adjacent to the living room.

He began using the washroom available in the master bed room of Daniel.

As a result, Daniel carried Bhagi to the farthest washroom every time Bhagi had a natural call. Apart from that, Daniel was forced to stand in front of Bhagi like a security guard to safeguard him from an unlikely ambush of a non-existent cockroach. Resultantly, Daniel underwent the ordeal of witnessing obscene acts like pissing, etc., of a six-year-old.

The nightmarish situation was wearing on Daniel's patience.

Chapter 13

RAM ARRIVED

8 A.M.

Payal and Aditya were waiting in Aditya's house for a constable who was expected to come in a mufti.

Payal contacted Sankar and informed that she was ready to leave in search of Bhagi.

"You continue your hunt. Keep as many copies of Bhagi photos as possible with you," Sankar guided. "The SI updated me that he deputed a constable along with a sniffer dog without a police collar belt. They will reach you anytime.

"The constable is asked to go in mufti. His name is Sri Ramachandra Murthy!

"Both of you comb the apartment complexes. Check whether anyone was leading an isolated life. Check for the yellow scooter.

"I hope you may be able to come up with some critical clues today."

"One more thing! If Daulat has called you anytime and warned you to return from the location where you're, please inform me immediately. It means, the kidnapper saw you. He alerted Daulat and Daulat in turn warned you to return! It means you are proximate to the kidnapper. We need to act fast from such a moment. I've deputed two constables in search of Noel."

Payal thanked Sankar.

*****

At around 9 a.m. a forty-year-old man in loose Teri cotton pants and double loose cotton shirt reached Aditya's house. He wore a mask. A dog was next to him. The dog seemed to be aged and crossed its retirement age in the police department. The man was carrying a polythene bag. He was Mr. Ramachandra Murthy who had come from the police department to assist Payal.

Payal received him and offered a glass of water.

In a mild protesting voice, he said," I've not done breakfast yet!"

"Oh! I'm sorry! Please come in!" said Payal and welcomed Ramachandra Murthy. The dog followed. It was not chained nor had a police collar belt.

Aditya's mother arranged breakfast for Murthy.

Ramachandra Murthy kept the polythene bag on a sofa. Aditya's mother shifted the bag to a corner on the floor close to the sofa.

Murthy stated in a grave voice, "That cover contains dog's food. Dog is a Rottweiler breed. The breed is hyper hygiene conscious; its food is to be kept securely in respectable places! That's why I've kept the bag on the sofa!"

Payal and Aditya felt amused.

Aditya relocated the polythene cover onto the sofa in a hurry. The dog lay on the floor and was watching the incident mutedly.

Murthy had breakfast to his heart's content and belched. He gulped a bottle of chilled water and burped twice.

Payal and Aditya sat across from him at the dining table.

"Is food packed for lunch?" Murthy had a poser.

"Yes! Yes! I've packed." Payal replied.

She was primed to start the pursuit of Bhagi as early as possible.

"I don't eat rice. Trust, you packed enough rolls of *Jowar Rotis*. City is under lockdown. We should not starve!" Ram declared.

"I've packed Spencer's Bread!" Payal answered anxiously.

Murthy raised the volume of his voice, "No! No! Bread is not to be consumed during Coronavirus times."

He took out his phone and selected a video and lectured, "WHO released this video last night to all governments. A scientist advised us to avoid rice, wheat, barley, and maize which were claimed to be the catalysts for the spread of Corona!" The mention of a scientist and the World Health Organisation shunned further questions on the subject.

Aditya's mother looked bewildered and was worried whether she would be summoned to prepare *Jowar Rotis.* She had not liked the idea of making *Jowar Rotis* at that hour.

Everyone looked at her. She nervously said, "I don't think I've *Jowar Atta*!"

Murthy surprised everyone, "I saw Aasheerwad *Jowar* Super Fine *Atta* cover in the dust bin at the front gate of your house! Please note I'm from the Crime Intelligence department!"

Aditya's mom retracted swiftly, "Yes! Yes! I remember now! I have *Jowar Atta.* Give me just ten minutes!" She staggered into the kitchen. She felt so annoyed that she thought she would congest dozens of *Jowar Rotis* into the mouth of Murthy at once, so that not only he but none in his family would get Coronavirus!

Payal felt the episode amusing. She doubted whether she got stuck with a melodramatic police constable to work with!

Jowar rotis were received from the kitchen after an hour.

The time was 10.30 a.m.

Payal started the car. She was in a hurry to begin her mission!

Murthy slumped in the seat next to Payal with a *Jowar roti* packet secured on his lap.

The dog was waiting and didn't yet get into the rear seat. It was growling. It was anxiously peering into the house. Ramchandra Murthy forgot its food cover on the sofa. Aditya came and gave the polythene cover to Murhty and said, "You forgot the dog's food on the sofa!" Murthy smiled sheepishly.

The dog, then, got into the rear seat.

Murthy preserved the dog's food cover at his feet in the car.

Payal muttered to herself, "*He brainwashed us by stating the dog will not eat its food if it is kept at disrespectable and unhygienic places; he placed the cover now at his feet, while he securely held the Jowar roti cover on his lap!*"

She said aloud, "Sir! Please place the dog's food in the rear seat! You will have more legroom and feel comfortable!"

"It's a ravenous eater!" Murthy replied. "Food is to be kept away from it. Let's go!"

Payal drove the car from Aditya's house.

"Hi, Sri Ramachandra Murthy! Are you from Hyderabad?" Payal eased into a chat to forge a workable relationship with a person who was going to be her associate in a critical activity.

"You may call me 'Ram'. I myself have forgotten my full name long ago. My parents named me Kausalya Dasaratha

Nandana Sri Ramachandra Murthy! When I joined school, my friends deleted 'Kausalya.' At college, my girlfriends deleted 'Dasaratha Nandana'.

"My colleagues abbreviated it as 'Ram' after joining the police department.

"Well! I've been in the Intelligence wing of the Police department for a long time. One cannot afford to have a sweet, long and soft name like 'Sri Ramachandra Murthy' and yet expect to deal with the underworld goons. In the crime department, the information should flow at rocket speed. If the informer has to call me by my full name, the crime would be over by the time he completes calling such a long name! So, I told my colleagues to call me 'Ram'." Murthy replied with a spark of wisdom in his eyes.

Payal endorsed, "Yup! The name 'Ram' is perfect for your profession."

Payal could not avoid looking at Ram's dress and fitness. 'Except name, rest of the features are out of date,' she felt.

She got tickled and felt like asking him whether his wife had not interfered with the balance of three alphabets left in his name after the marriage?

The sniffer dog began to snore in no time!

Payal enquired, "What is the dog's name?"

Ram clinically answered, "Laxman!"

4 P.M.

Payal and Ram had visited ten apartment complexes till then. Wherever they went they met the President or the Secretary of the Association and showed the photo of Bhagi. They posed a few common questions. They searched for a yellow chetak scooter in the parking areas and the cellar.

Ram was not liking this tedious approach.

They reached the gateway of another colony.

Ram reluctantly stood under a tree on the sideways of the road. He was feeling weary and frustrated. Laxman was lazily close to him.

Payal enquired, "Ram, shall we go?"

Ram asked with a dry expression, "Where?"

"To the next apartment complex!" Payal replied and began to walk ahead.

Ram saw Ratnadeep Department Store opposite them. He recalled the missing case of a boy from a wealthy family that took place two years ago. He remembered how ACP Venkat unravelled the case by shortlisting the hobbies, tastes and the habits of the missing boy.

He was sure Payal was not aware of the details of the old case. He felt he should parade his talent by replicating the same approach in Bhagi's case. In fact, he was feeling lazy to walk along with Payal.

Ram shouted, "Ma'am! Please come here!"

Payal stopped, turned around and looked at Ram inquisitively.

"I got appreciation from the SP two years ago when I netted a missing boy in ten hours. Shall we apply the same strategy? It works!"

Payal grew curious, "If it's going to work, we should implement it immediately!"

Ram even spontaneously named the strategy and said to her, "It's called 'random investigation' in our department." He continued, "You merely observe what I'm going to do now. Follow me."

He sported dark glasses to appear like a super-cop, tightened the waist belt to make the loose shirt and trouser portray him shapely.

Ram strutted to the Ratnadeep Store. Payal followed. Laxman was made to sit at the doorway of the Store.

Ram called the supervisor of the store and said," I'm Ram from the crime department."

He showed the ID.

Payal was hesitantly and uncomfortably looking at Ram's swagger.

Ram showed the photo of Bhagi to the supervisor and he questioned in a demanding tone, "Is this boy seen here? He's missing. I want to examine your store's CCTV footage!"

Ram's ploy was he would settle down in front of the PC monitor going through the footage in the air-conditioned store while Payal would carry on the backbreaking search moving from flat to flat. Laxman would be left to enjoy its snooze at the entrance of the store.

The mention of the Crime Department sent ripples in the Store.

Ram turned to Payal and interrogatively questioned, "What food is most liked by Bhagi?"

Payal honestly replied, 'Ice cream!"

Payal had not imagined what was begun by Ram as a 'random investigation', which was like tossing a coin in the air, was going to take her to Daniel after five minutes!

"Which brand of ice cream does he like the most?" Ram cross-examined superlatively.

"Uh! Umm! Magnum Double Hot Chocolate!" Payal replied inescapably.

Ram commanded the supervisor with an air of authority, "Check if anyone bought Magnum Double Hot Chocolate from your store in the last 48 hours!"

There was a short queue at the store in the evening hours.

A cashier at the billing desk who was overhearing the conversation said, "Sir, one man has bought a Magnum Double Hot Chocolate tub just now. He has paid in cash and has not shared his phone number. He has just left holding the ice cream tub in a white carry bag."

Payal's eyes popped out with curiosity.

Ram felt like Sherlock Holmes and stared at Payal. He directed Payal, "I would take the pain of going through the CCTV footage. Meanwhile, you do me a favour. You pursue the man who bought ice cream five minutes ago!"

Payal had already dashed out of the store to look for a man carrying an ice cream tub.

At a distance of around two hundred metres, she discerned a man walking away from the store. There was something in his hand in white colour. He was turning right to enter another street. He was not visible now.

Payal parked the car two lanes away. She decided to run in the direction the man went and she reached the man. He wore a jeans trouser and a designer ethnic cotton shirt. He donned Nike shoes, a sun hat, a large mask and Rayban glasses. He was stylish.

Payal greeted, "Hi Sir!"

It was Daniel. He looked at Payal and was stunned to encounter Payal.

Payal saw a folded mini white umbrella in Daniel's hand. There was no white carry bag in his hand. Payal realised she mistook the folded white umbrella for a carry bag.

Payal asked, "Sir! Have you seen by chance a guy of around 30 years going in this direction with a white carry bag in his hand? He was carrying an ice cream tub!"

Daniel nodded. "Yes. One young fellow went in this direction on a yellow scooter. I saw a white carry bag clung to the handle. He turned to that left at the end of this lane." Daniel pointed his index finger to a spot in the opposite direction of his flat.

'Yellow Scooter!" Payal jumped over the moon. She sprinted in the direction shown by Daniel.

Daniel heaved a sigh of relief. He told himself," *What a narrow escape!*" He left that spot in a jiffy!

*****

On his way to the flat, he reminisced about the incident that happened a couple of minutes before Payal met him.

'I bought a Magnum Double Hot Chocolate tub for Bhagi at the Ratnadeep Store and was returning to my flat!

I walked two hundred metres from the store and took a right turn. A ten-year-old girl approached me. She stretched her hand begging for money.

A woman standing at a distance pleaded loudly, "Sir, please give some money to my daughter. We're labour from Bihar. Due to the lockdown, we're struggling to survive. Please help!"

I gave a five hundred rupee note to the girl. Her face lit up. She ambled towards a tractor flapping the five hundred rupees note jubilantly in the air.

The woman shouted, "Sofia! Run fast! The tractor is likely to go!"

I heard the name "Sofia!"

I called the girl, "Sofia! Come here!"

The girl returned to where I was standing. Her eyes dilated expecting more gifts.

"Is your name Sofia?" I questioned.

She said yes.

I gave the white carry bag with the ice cream tub to Sofia, gave her another five hundred rupees note and said, "Please go now!"

My eyes were filled with tears instantaneously. I became emotional for a moment.

My mother's name is Sofia!

Sofia turned back and waved at me. I waved back involuntarily. The tractor left with a load of migrant workers.

I watched Sofia as long as I could.

I told myself, I should go to the store once again to purchase a Magnum Double Hot Chocolate tub.

It was hot. I took the kerchief and wiped out the sweat.

I thought I would unfold the umbrella that I was carrying. I was about to unfold the umbrella. Payal came. I was stunned to see Payal. She enquired about a man carrying a white carry bag with an ice cream tub in it. I misdirected her.'

Daniel had decided not to go to the Ratnadeep store anymore.

*****

Payal drained her energy for the next two hours searching in the wrong locations for a man who bought Magnum

Double Hot Chocolate from the store. She could not find him. When she returned to the store, she found Ram in deep sleep wheezing in a chair in front of the CCTV monitor. A coca cola bottle and half a dozen Haldiram savoury packets were lying empty on the table. Laxman was idling like a retired government employee.

Payal searched on the CCTV to ascertain who had come two hours ago to the store to buy a Double Hot Chocolate Ice cream tub! She realised the man who misdirected her had bought the ice cream. His face was not visible. She noticed as he left the store, he carried a white carry bag and a white umbrella folded in his hands. She grasped she met the kidnapper a while ago! She wondered, '*When I met him, there was no ice cream bag in his hand! All the more, I'm unable to see his facial features as he wore a mask, a hat and dark glasses!*' She decided to search for him among the flats in the direction he might have gone!

Chapter 14

SENIOR POLICE OFFICERS HUDDLE

6 P.M.

A review was going on at the police headquarters, Hyderabad in regard to the lockdown situation. The DIG of Police, Hemachandar, was unhappy.

Sankar, ASP, was part of the review along with many DSPs and ASPs in the city.

Hemachandar highlighted a few examples of the police excesses peddled by the TV media.

He said, "Media and social media are alleging that many excesses are perpetrated by the police in the name of lockdown.

"It was claimed a fifty-year-old teacher was brutally beaten to death by the police for the reason he was roaming without wearing a mask.

"The media claimed he wore a mask. He was said to be going to a hospital to undergo a Coronavirus test.

"A video showing a police inspector pulling the old man from the bike to the ground was also being circulated. The mask went off his face when he fell down from the bike.

"The police inspector beat him ruthlessly for not wearing a mask. Later on, he died, the media alleged.

"The video has been going viral for the last twenty-four hours. The local police had a different version. They stated they stopped him for not wearing a mask. The police inspector offered him a mask. The old man was not well and he fell down from the bike and died, the police said. The police cited his weak health and corona virus infection as reasons for the death while social media and the TV media accused the police.

"In this background, I was instructed by our Commissioner to conduct a conference and review.

"Our Commissioner is furious with our approach. It has been three or four days since lockdown was imposed in Telangana state and the talk of excesses by the police already hit the air. The CM called the senior police officials and held a meeting. He regarded CoronaVirus as an unprecedented event impacting the lives of the common people, the migrant labour, the middle class and the sick as never heard before. The CM said he had not liked the approach of the police and wanted us to evaluate. The reputation of the police department is at stake."

Pin drop silence prevailed in the conference hall.

One ASP suggested, "Sir! Shall we organise free food for the poor!"

An officer proposed distribution of masks and sanitizers free of cost.

Another officer proposed donation of blood by all the police staff across the state!

Hemachandar replied disappointedly, "You guys are not getting the point! Free food, free clothes, free water, free masks, freebies, donations of blood and food are not what I'm talking about.

"The city is down and is on its knees.

"We should organise something transformational to cheer up the soul of the city. It's to be something like where all classes of people should feel inspired. We need to bring a sense of harmony! Think of something on those lines. The Chief Commissioner gave us one-day time! It's to be organised fast. Organising such an initiative at the end of the lockdown has no relevance."

After the conclusion of the review meeting, Sankar was returning to his station located in Madhapur.

The vehicle was crossing Madhapur church. A mellifluous voice singing a melody of SPB was echoing through a mic. The song was coming from the lane opposite to the church. Sankar recognized the voice of the singer. It was Noel's voice.

He asked the driver to stop the vehicle, lowered the window glasses and looked in the direction of the department store. He saw Noel!

He got down from the vehicle and walked over to the store.

A parasol, table, chair and a microphone were seen by Sankar. Noel sat under the parasol.

Sankar felt exuberant at finding Noel. He texted Payal and Rama Sastry that Noel was found.

Noel saw Sankar and stood up nervously.

Sankar requested him to relax and focus on the song. He saw the cheering crowd around Noel. He learnt from the Manager of the store the extent of popularity that Noel gained on social media!

'Noel-a prodigy! A born musician! An orphan! A self-made virtuoso!' remarks were galore on social media!

Noel played the latest song they uploaded on the podcast by name "Strings".

Sankar was awestruck. He could feel Goosebumps of joy! He scrolled on his mobile phone and found streams of messages about Noel on social media. He cursed himself for being so busy with office work that he did not notice the messages about Noel!

An idea struck Sankar!

He requested his boss that the police department may adopt Noel as their child and nourish his talent! And the news of adoption was to be announced by the Police Commissioner.

He shot a video of Noel while he was singing and playing on guitar and posted to Hemachandar on WhatsApp. He shared the popular messages about Noel on social media with Hemachandar. He informed him that Noel was an orphan!

He also called Hemachandar to seek permission to organise an open concert at Durgam Cheruvu Cable bridge.

Hemachandar was thrilled at the idea of adoption of an orphan and a music prodigy. The new Durgam Cheruvu bridge was due for inauguration and was not open for public use and it was the ideal location to hold the concert during the lockdown.

He requisitioned Sankar to bring the members of the 'Strings' unit to his chambers the next day.

*****

Sankar asked Noel, "Where have you stayed the last two nights?"

Noel informed that he slept in the church premises.

Sankar invited him to his house.

*****

Sankar informed Payal about the plan to organise a music concert by the unit of "Strings" at Durgam Cheruvu Cable Bridge to be live telecast on all channels.

"Oh! Great! On what date?" Payal asked.

"It will be on the 28th of this month. From 5 pm to 7 pm! The DIG has just given permission. I'm sure media channels would do a live telecast if Hemachandar takes the initiative. It would rock the city! Our DIG requested me to bring the Unit tomorrow to his chambers. I will take Aditya, Sandhya and Noel to the DIG's office."

Payal sent a flying kiss to Sankar.

Chapter 15

DANIEL'S ORDEALS CONTINUED

27TH MARCH 2020

8 A.M.

Daniel was exhausted by the incessant service that he was rendering to Bhagi.

He was charming the distinguished guest by laboriously playing video games along with him.

He too operated racing cars.

He purposely veered an animated racing car against a wall or hit a vehicle or killed pedestrians in the Cross Road game.

Bhagi steered the car with ease and tutored Daniel how easy it was!

Bhagi was made to be the everlasting champion. Unparallel winning gave kick to him.

In that intoxicated swagger, he blurted that one day he would hunt a real tiger and he would finish it off with his left hand.

Daniel began administering sleeping pills and sedative syrups to keep Bhagi drowsy.

*****

Daulat confirmed to Daniel he was sure to get cash on the 28th morning.

Daniel cautioned, "Daulat! You're saying pleasant things to me over the phone. But you cunningly sent Payal, your sister, in search of me! After seeing her, I thought I should kill your son! I want to give you one last chance!"

Daulat trembled and pleaded, "Sir! I'm swearing. I've not sent Payal. I've asked her to leave my flat when I've learnt that she has taken police support. Please trust me. My wife and I are with you. We're trying our best to mislead Payal.

"Payal has contacted my accountant to inquire about any large withdrawals of cash from my firm's account. The accountant is my right hand and is groomed by me. I told my accountant to misguide Payal.

"I'm doing all these things with absolute trust in you. Please don't do any harm to my son. Just one more day to close our deal.

"I will right now contact Payal and warn her to come back from where she is!"

Daniel angered, "Don't call her back. It will serve as a hint to Payal that you and I are in contact. It will be suicidal for us.

"You arrange the cash on priority." Daniel decreed and cut the call.

Chapter 16

SANKAR GOT DIG'S NOD TO ORGANIZE THE CONCERT

10 A.M.

It was the police headquarters, Hyderabad.

"Strings" was a private album composed by Payal, Aditya and Sandhya. The theme had revolved around the social and financial issues faced by the orphans. After Noel's entry, the song, the script, the tune and its rhyme got a heavenly touch so much so that Payal had christened the unit's name itself as "Strings".

The 'Strings' Unit, except Payal, had been waiting outside the chambers of DIG Hemachander. Sankar accompanied them to introduce to Hemachandar.

Hemachandar welcomed the 'Strings' unit and listened to the songs of Noel, Aditya and Sandhya.

After listening to Noel, he persuasively said, "We're going to host this music concert tomorrow."

Noel, Aditya and Sandhya thanked the DIG and left his office.

Hemachander instructed Sankar, "Two critical points. One is that our department shall sponsor the live music concert. Secondly, we shall adopt Noel. It shall salvage our repute.

"Organise the event on Durgam Cheruvu cable bridge tomorrow from 5 p.m. to 7 p.m. Give admission to the three musicians. None from the family or friends shall be allowed.

"Media persons to be given admission to facilitate live telecast.

"The Commissioner will do a 'virtual' inauguration and formally address the TV audience.

"Deck up the Cable bridge with lighting.

"Arrange the best microphones to the unit.

"Escort Noel and his team in your own official vehicle to the venue.

"Arrange a write up on the program. Organise an anchor and enliven the show.

"Grand publicity should be arranged on all channels, social media in the next 24 hours. I will take care of it.

"I will request the Commissioner to contact singer S.P. Bala Subramanyam (SPB) and seek his foreword about the concert."

"After the concert, you will personally drop Noel, Aditya and Sandhya at their residence.

"You check with them what more assistance they need!

"Social distancing" is mandatory among all including the members of the 'Strings' unit.

"Keep sanitizers handy!"

Sankar was scribbling fast on a notepad while Hemachandar listed out the agenda.

Sankar showed the picture of Payal on the phone to Hemachandar and informed she was the writer of the song which was sung by Noel.

He said that the song was liked by none other than SPB and he himself had appreciated it on social media after which the song had captured the attention of millions!

Hemachandar asked why had Payal not come to meet him?

Sankar said she was preoccupied with important domestic work and would meet him at the earliest.

*****

From 1 p.m. onwards, Telugu TV news channels began to give publicity about the next day's live telecast of the concert.

It was communicated, the show was not open to the public and no tickets would be sold. The concert could only be watched 'live' on television channels.

At 9 p.m. the media released thirty second video footage of SPB conveying his best wishes to the Police Department and the unit of "Strings" for their upcoming concert on 28th evening. The message by the music wizard sent the news viral.

*****

2 P.M.

Sankar contacted Payal and updated her about the fast developments in regard to the stage show by 'Strings' unit on 28th evening. She thanked him for the excellent lift that her unit was likely to receive after the show!

"Where are you now?" Sankar enquired Payal.

"I'm with constable Ram. We're about to meet the President of the owners' association of Rosewood Apartments."

Payal moved away from constable Ram and spoke in a low voice, "Sankar! Daulat is going to meet the kidnapper and settle the ransom amount on 29th at 3 P.M."

"29th! Day after tomorrow! Is the venue of their meeting known?" Sankar queried curiously.

"No. Not yet. Will let you know. Sneha promised to inform me!"

Daulat asked Sneha to misinform Payal that the ransom amount was going to be exchanged with the kidnapper on 29th March. The actual date was 28th March!! Sneha, now, was more concerned about her son's safe return than being honest to Payal!

Chapter 17

RAM AND PAYAL BUMPED INTO DANIEL

3 P.M.

Ram was indifferently standing under the roof of a medical Store in a by-lane. His forehead wore convulsive folds and he was often twitching his eyes-a sign of tiresomeness.

Payal was trying to fix the next flat to be visited.

They had just come out of the Rosewood Apartment complex.

Ram had not brought sniffer dog Laxman on day two of the investigation.

He reluctantly followed Payal as she briskly walked toward a newly built apartment complex.

*****

Daniel was noticing through the narrowly opened window of his flat.

Both Payal and Ram were walking towards his flats' complex.

Daniel was ready for such eventuality.

He briskly put on an expensive white cotton full hand shirt and a white *lungi* with a grandly designed border.

He applied *Vibhuti* across his forehead.

He took out a plastic wire bag containing a dozen miniature brass pots. The pots were already garnished with Hindu religion auspicious signs around them. The pots were sealed.

He twisted a cotton towel into the shape of a headgear and fixed it on his head and wore a Coronavirus mask on his face.

He scrutinised himself in the mirror. He seemed like a pious Hindu gentleman. He looked at Bhagi. He was in a deep sleep after being given sleeping pills.

He came down to the ground floor with a mission to distract Payal.

Payal and Ram entered the complex and at the entrance, they met Daniel.

Payal greeted him and asked, "Sir, may we come in!"

Daniel said, "Please Ma'am!" He slightly modified the timbre of his voice and softened his tone to discourage Payal from recognizing his voice.

Payal introduced herself and conveyed her need to meet the President of the Owners Association.

Daniel himself accompanied Payal and Ram to the President's flat.

President Venkata Swamy was pleased to see Daniel and said, "Rama Rao! How are you? Who are these two?" (For the apartment dwellers, Daniel's name was Rama Rao and he is an insurance agent.)

All the four stood five to six feet apart and managed social distancing!

Payal introduced herself to Venkata Swamy and politely showed the photo of Bhagi. She enquired whether the boy was seen anywhere?

She asked three mandatory questions, "Sir! Any bachelor residing in your flats? Has anyone joined the flats recently? Anyone in the age group of.......?" Payal had not completed the sentence. Daniel intercepted her flow tactfully.

He opened the plastic wire bag. He brought out three brass pots and said, "Sirs! Please accept one pot each. My wife's uncle went to Kasi. He returned last week. Holy water of the Ganges is inside the pots. It's crucial to keep a brass pot of the river Ganges at home. No virus would dare come in!"

The faces of Venkata Swamy and Ram brightened the way Sachin Tendulkar's face would glow when the bowler bowled a juicy half volley at him when he was on 99!

All the three have received the pots.

Payal was about to keep it in her trouser pocket.

Ram precipitously objected, "Ma'am! No! No! You need to hold the pot gracefully in your hands with both palms around the pot!"

Payal felt embarrassed. She inattentively shook the pot to feel its contents!

Ram looked heartbroken! He disagreeably lamented, "I cannot say how much your generation is not aware of the power of the river Ganges! Please, for God's sake, don't play with it! Never ever try to open the seal. The water can be preserved for centuries if the seal is not opened. It will not evaporate!!"

Payal sheepishly stared at everyone.

Venkata Swamy thanked Daniel alias *Rama Rao* for the holy water.

He turned to Payal and answered," Uh! Um! There is not a single bachelor in our apartments. We're a bunch of disciplined owners and tenants."

Payal left the photo of Bhagi with Venkata Swamy.

Daniel said to Venkata Swamy, "Sir! I'm going down to place a few pots at the entrance gate! It will work wonders!" Venkata Swamy thanked Daniel.

Payal and Ram returned to the ground floor.

Daniel followed them chanting pious hymns. He said, "Today, all luck is yours. You're destined to receive the sacred water!"

Ram thanked, "True. We're fortunate. Having the possession of the Ganges holy water is like Lord Shiva himself arriving and standing by us to fight Corona! *Om! Namah! Sivaya*!"

Payal had not lost focus. She went to the cellar and searched for the yellow-coloured two-wheeler.

She had not seen a yellow scooter.

Payal and Ram were convinced, there was nothing for them to suspect. They thanked Daniel and left.

*****

Payal did not find the yellow Chetak scooter in the cellar because Daniel parked the scooter in the parking area of a Sub Registrar government office premises three lanes away from the house.

Even if Payal and Ram happened to enter the Sub Registrar office premises by chance or with a pinch of suspicion, they would have found a Chetak scooter but not a yellow-coloured Chetak!

Daniel used the spray paint cans and changed the colour of the Chetak from Yellow to Brown colour on the night of 25th March. It had just taken half an hour to spray the paint!

5 P.M.

Ram said tediously, "Ma'am! Shall we continue tomorrow!"

Payal thought she should first get rid of Ram. She drove the car to the police station.

When they reached Madhapur police station, Payal took out Rs.5000 from the purse, thrusted it into Ram's pocket and said, "Thanks for the support. My friend is going to join me tomorrow. You take a break."

Ram thanked Payal and got down the car.

Payal, while reversing the car, observed that Ram forgot the brass pot on the dashboard.

She called Ram.

She handed the pot to him and asked, "Have you forgotten the holy water?!"

Ram had a ready excuse, "For a moment, my mind got fixed on Lord Shiva! In that divine moment, I forget myself! Thanks a lot!"

He walked away holding the pot reverently.

Chapter 18

JAGGU LOSES A FIGHT BUT FINDS A FORTUNE

28TH MARCH 2020

8 A.M.

"It's a unique occasion for us. This evening, Noel is participating in a prestigious music concert. Due to lockdown restrictions, we're not allowed to go to the Cable Bridge. The performance is going to be telecast live from 5 to 7 p.m. on TV. We shall watch the telecast together. I want Jaggu to reach home before 5 p.m.," Rama Sastry communicated to the boys at the Tapaswi Home.

The boys were in an excited mood.

Sastry was being appreciated on all TV media channels for having given shelter to Noel, and helped him realise his dream.

Sastry was honest as ever. He said to the Press reporters it was Sankar and Payal who were the chief patrons of Noel. He even mentioned the name of Late Janaki Ram, father of Daulat and thanked Daulat's family for the land that they donated to Tapaswi Home.

Daulat was watching Rama Sastry on TV. He felt Sastry was attempting to exploit the opportunity and involve the Media in his plan to continue at the site. He was more annoyed that Sankar and Payal were providing Rama Sastry requisite support.

8.30 A.M.

Payal was about to leave Aditya's house in her pursuit of Bhagi.

She conveyed best wishes to Aditya and Sandhya. Aditya and Sandhya had mixed feelings. On one side they were happy they were going to perform their first live show. On the other hand, Payal might not be part of the show.

Payal confessed, "I'm feeling odd at the contrasting sides of two events taking place in my life at the same time! My dream project is going to be launched by way of a music concert today. I'm sad I'm not going to be part of it. I'm busy searching for my nephew and I'm sure to crack it anytime."

Aditya requested her, "I guess you can join the concert. It starts at 5 p.m. For today, you may wind up searching for Bhagi and join the live concert!"

Payal promised she would consider it and drove out of Aditya's house.

Noel was at Sankar's residence. Sankar was to drop him at Aditya's residence for rehearsals.

Payal was driving the car. She contacted Sankar to brief him what she had planned for the day.

"Sankar, I will continue my search. I covered more or less eighty percent of the flats surrounding our Sahiti complex. I told you about the ice cream incident. I'm sure the kidnapper is somewhere near us. I happened to meet him on that day. A young chap and very stylish guy.

"News is Daulat set cash ready to exchange it with the kidnapper tomorrow at 3 p.m. The venue for their meeting was our Madhapur sweet retail shop premises! Before the cash is handed over, we shall nab him!"

Sankar assured her, "Yes! You're likely to make a breakthrough even before. I'm tied up with the live show today. I request you too to be part of the show. It's like a once in a lifetime event for a budding music unit like yours. Don't miss it!

"You should reach the venue before 5 p.m. to lead the music concert."

Payal said, "Sure!"

*****

8.15 A.M. TO 2 P.M

Except Jaggu, the rest of the boys of the Tapaswi Home had nowhere to go.

Social Welfare schools were shut down. Part time jobs were lost due to Coronavirus and resultant lockdown.

The story of Jaggu was different. He had not lost his job during Corona turbulence.

Sastry requested him not to go for the job on that specific day. He wanted every inmate of Tapaswi Home to watch Noel's live performance today. Jaggu said he could not afford to take one-day leave.

If it was found, he had been absent for one day, his area of operation would be poached by someone else.

It was a fight for survival.

Jaggu left Tapaswi Home by 8.15 a.m.

He traversed the next ten kilometres across narrow alleys. He strode alongside the city's filthy roads and raced ahead crossing the footpaths and the slums.

He had not halted a single minute anywhere. While he criss-crossed through the narrow alleys and shortcuts, he had not flinched an inch when he waded through the nauseating smell of the slums.

It was 10 a.m. by the time Jaggu reached the outskirts of the city.

He swung into action straightaway. His eyes were prying sharply to acquire as much as he could, as fast as he could!

Khalif was his chief adversary.

Khalif spotted Jaggu from a distance. He came running to him. Many boys and girls noticed Khalif running towards Jaggu. They anticipated a street brawl. It was a feast for them.

All the boys and girls converged to where Khalif and Jaggu were about to have a fight.

Khalif mocked Jaggu, "Noel was doing well now! Why are you still coming to this place? You can now leave your area to me."

Jaggu retorted, "If Noel makes money, it's for himself. My life is different."

Khalif intentionally insulted, "You're a greedy pig!"

Khalif provokingly threw a piece of sharp stone at him. It hit Jaggu in his face. Jaggu lost his cool.

Khalif and Jaggu declared a one-on-one joust.

Others were divided into two sides. They began to clap and encourage them to fight.

Habitually, Jaggu would win. Majority of the boys were betting on Jaggu. A few hardcore gamblers betted on Khaliff.

Khalif punched a fierce blow into the lower jaw of Jaggu.

Jaggu fell backwards. He lost control and was unable to hold onto anything!

He began to roll down from the top of a garbage mound.

It was the city's garbage dumping yard located on the outskirts. Jaggu and Khalif would collect trash like tins, glass and other metal material and sell the trash to scrap traders!

Jaggu and Khalif had a fight on top of the garbage yard which was as high as a five-storey building! Jaggu was descending unabated upside down. He tried hard to restrain himself from skidding downhill. He went down as if someone were pushing him from the top.

He went to the bottom of the garbage mound and his head hit the floor. He was upside down. He was bleeding through the nose. His heart was pounding heavily. He did a somersault to get to normal position. He looked up.

Khalif and the gang could be seen at the top. They were laughing madly.

Those who betted in favour of Khalif were collecting money from the fans of Jaggu!

Jaggu scoured his back for the gunny bag in which he secured the items of trash that he was collecting at the garbage. The bag was not at its normal position. He lost it somewhere while he was skidding downwards.

He combed wildly for his gunny bag amidst the garbage.

He saw a bag with Lord Balaji logo five feet away. It looked similar to the bag he carried on his back on that day.

He drew the bag near to him. The gunny bag was tied tight. He felt curious.

He untied the bag and found trash inside. He thrusted his hand and groped. He felt a bundle. He drew it out. A bundle of Rs.2000 currency notes came into his hand. He was astonished. He peeped into the bag and saw five bundles altogether. He did not know how much value it could be. He understood it would be running into lakhs of rupees of cash.

Jaggu looked around. His hands were shivering with panic as he never saw such a huge amount of cash.

None was present there.

None could risk walking into such a steeply treacherous corner amidst a mountain of garbage.

A bulldozer of Greater Hyderabad Municipal Corporation might plough in from any side any moment, pluck him with its giant sized shovel braced with sharp teeth and pulp him into pieces along with other trash. There would not be any trace of his body. Noise of bulldozers and tippers were being heard in the vicinity.

He swiftly thrusted the cash bundles back into the old gunny bag. He puffed trash around the cash. He tied the mouth of the bag tight. He started running towards Tapaswi Home.

He gleefully thanked Khalif for that strong blow which hit him!

He forgot the pain of the blow.

He did not mind a bleeding nose.

He loved to forgive Khalif!!

Money was sweet. It could overrule all impediments in life!!

He was feeling nervous when a gunny bag with lakhs of worth cash was dangling on his back. He felt the Almighty might have sent the cash.

He decided he would deliver the cash to Rama Sastry and request him to use the cash for purchase of a permanent home for Tapaswi Home!

*****

2 P.M.

Jaggu reached Tapaswi Home. He was sweating enormously. Everyone welcomed Jaggu and cheered him for having returned home well before the scheduled hour.

Jaggu went to Rama Sastry and whispered in his ears. Sastry was taking a nap and he sat up surprised.

Jaggu handed the gunny bag to Sastry. Both went inside the shed and closed the doors.

Sastry opened the bag, carted the cash bundles and spread them on the floor. He astonishingly said, "It's one crore! Where have you found the cash?"

Jaggu narrated the entire episode.

"Why did you get inclined to open this specific bag among so much trash when you were searching for your own gunny bag?"

'Last week, I brought two old gunny bags from the TTD office. Both were of the same colour and had the logo of Lord Balaji! I kept the bags in our home. Next day, I found one bag was missing. I was using the other bag.

"I lost it when I skidded off the top of the dump yard. When I was searching for my bag, I saw this bag with Lord

Balaji logo in the dump yard. I became naturally curious, involuntarily opened the bag and found the cash!

"Sir, please use this money to purchase a new home for us. God has sent the money to us."

Rama Sastry went speechless. He felt proud of Jaggu's attitude. The boy did not run away with the cash. Instead, he offered the money to be used for the purchase of a new home for all of them!!

Sastry recalled Daulat coming to Tapaswi home one afternoon and taking away a gunny bag! This was the same bag!

He contacted Sankar.

Sankar responded, "Sir! How are you? Good afternoon! You must be a happy man! Your decades of efforts are culminating into a fruitful mega event today!"

"Good afternoon, Sankar! It's not my effort alone. Without you this would not have been possible!"

"Sir, tell me what can I do for you?"

"Could we meet tonight at Tapaswi Home after the concert? Jaggu found a gunny bag with cash. If you remember, I informed you a few days ago that Daulat had come to Tapaswi Home and took with him an old gunny bag!"

"Oh! Is it? How much cash is it?"

"One crore!"

"Oh my god! Will surely reach there before 8 p.m. tonight!"

"I guess the cash belonged to Daulat. I need your help to return it to him."

"We will discuss it tonight!" Sankar assured.

Sastry kept the cash in a wooden trunk box and locked it. After fifteen years of the foundation of the orphanage, the trunk box was locked for the first time!

Chapter 19

DANIEL AND DAULAT FINALISE THE VENUE TO EXCHANGE BHAGI AND CASH

4 P.M.

Daulat was pleased with the progress of the day so far for four reasons.

First reason was, since Payal was not residing with him in the same flat, he could step out of the house without being tracked by her.

Secondly, the chairman of the cooperative bank door-delivered Rs. one crore cash as promised.

Thirdly, Daniel verified the cash through a WhatsApp video half an hour ago and he was satisfied.

Fourthly and importantly, Daniel disclosed to Daulat to which location and at what time the money should be brought.

*****

Daniel too was pleased with the progress during the day.

He called Daulat, instructed seven steps to be adhered to by himself and Daulat. He ordered Daulat to note down the seven steps.

***Step 1**: Daulat is to come to Lord Shiva temple at 7 p.m. There is a Shiva temple one kilometre from Daulat's house.*

(Daniel has thought it will be risky to execute the plan during the day time. He has remembered the incident behind Kamala Mall)

***Step 2**: Daniel too will reach Lord Shiva temple on the scooter by 7. P.M. in the form of a temple priest. (Daniel has decided it will be safe if he has gone wearing a Hindu priest's dress code to Shiva temple. None will bother to suspect a temple priest.) Daniel will not bring Bhagi to Shiva temple. (Bhagi is the insurance against any risk of complaint to the police by Daulat)*

***Step 3:** Daniel will receive ransom money from Daulat at the Shiva temple.*

***Step 4:** Daniel will return to the flat and verify the genuineness of currency.*

***Step 5:** Daulat will return to Sahiti Complex and will wait for Daniel's next phone call.*

***Step 6:** Daniel, after being satisfied with the cash, will drop Bhagi at a location which he will reveal to Daulat over phone. If there is any discrepancy of any nature in the cash, Bhagi will be murdered.*

***Step 7**: Daulat is to reach the location where Bhagi is dropped by Daniel and receive his son!*

Step 8 and Step 9 are to be adhered solely by Daniel, drafted by Daniel and kept with himself.

Step 8: *'After being satisfied with the cash, I will drop Bhagi at his school lane. I will tie him to a tree in the lane. I will call Daulat and inform that Bhagi is tied to a tree at the school. Before Daulat has reached the school, I will leave the place.*

Step 10: *I will remove the SIM and throw it into the sewerage.'*

There would be no trace of any trail of kidnap, he surmised.

Chapter 20

THE GRAND MUSIC CONCERT AT DURGAM CHERUVU

4.00 P.M.

Durgam Cheruvu Cable bridge cables and piers were decorated with ornamental bunting banners; long artificial flower garlands were hung from top to the floor of the bridge.

Tri coloured balloons were hung wonderfully decorating the steel ropes lying on both sides of the cable bridge.

Lighting was magnificently done with serial light strips being suspended in loops all over the buildings, trees and poles adjacent to the cable bridge. And the bridge was illuminated with lighting which would dazzle when twilight had set in.

The National Flag was fluttering quietly amidst the celebrative occasion. The setting was ready for the live music show to start.

Sankar had reached the venue along with Aditya, Noel and Sandhya. Payal promised to reach soon.

An open dais was set up covered with red coloured carpet for Noel, Payal Aditya and Sandhya. Microphones and speakers were arranged.

There was a large LED screen at the location for visual displays. Messages of celebrities of the twin cities with their brief messages were being telecast on the screen conveying their best wishes to the music Unit.

Images of the Chief Commissioner of Police handing over appreciation certificates to the doctors of the city were being displayed on the screen.

Videos of the Home Minister speaking to the migrant labour and educating them about the facilities arranged by the government during the pandemic were being telecast on the screen.

Images of the popular NGOs distributing food, clothes, masks, sanitizers and water to the poorer sections of the society were being exhibited.

Photos of the Chief Minister handing over appreciation letters and bank cheques to some of the sanitary workers who had shown exemplary discipline and commitment during this period were shown on the screen.

Police band was playing patriotic songs.

There were a dozen police staff, half a dozen media personnel and three musicians and the choir of the police band, and Assistant Superintendent of Police-Sankar at the venue.

Payal was not able to make any breakthrough in her search for Bhagi. She made it to the venue on time. Aditya set the *tabla* instrument. Sandhya was to operate the keyboard. Noel sat with a guitar. Payal conducted and unified the orchestra.

The proceedings were being telecast live.

Hemachandar came on the LED screen. He announced the names of the official sponsors of the program and thanked them.

The Commissioner of Police appeared on the screen. He thanked veteran singer SP Balasubramanyam for sparing his valuable time and lent his foreword to the program.

He announced that Noel was adopted by the police department.

At 5 p.m. on dot, the concert took off.

Noel offered prayer to the Almighty. There was pin drop silence at the venue. The rustling noise of breeze, cackling sounds of balloons, bunting papers, serial light strips were adding jubilation to the event.

The dais was set in the middle of the road at the entrance of the Cable Bridge.

Millions of viewers were watching the live telecast.

Millions of feelings were aspiring to see a vibrant music show alleviating their moods which were drowned in the gloominess of Corona suffering.

Millions of hearts were racing with millions of expectations when a thirteen-year-old boy by name Noel stood up in front of the microphone with a guitar in his hands.

The names of Payal, Aditya, Sandhya and Noel had become household names in the last twenty-four hours.

Noel felt the picture of SPB that was bonded on the face of the guitar!

He started the program with a Telugu song by SP Bala Subramanyam!

He followed it up with countless soul-stirring songs from SPB! Hindi songs of Mukesh, Kishore Kumar and Rafi followed!

Two hours went by in a moment.

At the end, Payal, Aditya and Sandhya thanked the Police department and the government for adopting Noel!

They conveyed special thanks to the audience for subscribing to their channel and for encouraging them in such a big way!! They thanked SPB for providing them a platform!

Sankar gave mementos to the four.

The program was closed at 7 p.m.

Five minutes later, Sankar, Aditya, Sandhya, Payal and Noel left the venue in the police van. Aditya and Sandhya were dropped at Aditya's residence and Sankar, Payal and Noel proceeded to Tapaswi Home.

Chapter 21

ANTI CLIMAX

7 P.M.

A Hindu temple priest-aged around 28 years, in a bare upper body with a white *Dhoti* tied around the waist, a sacred thread looped over the shoulders across the chest going under the opposite arm, having applied *Vibhuti* on the shoulders, the chest, the forehead and with Sindhuram at the centre of the junction between his nose and the eyes, with a mala of Rudraksha beads around the neck- came on a brown coloured scooter to the Shiva temple. He was Daniel. Daulat was already there waiting for him. The temple was closed and there was none in that lane. Daulat handed the leather bag containing Rs. one crore cash. Daniel opened the bag and found bundles of cash. Before leaving he said, "Daulat, I will call you within twenty minutes. You go back to your complex and wait there."

7.25 P.M.

Daulat was waiting for more than twenty minutes in the parking area of Sahithi Complex. By this time, he should have received the call from Daniel. All these days, he was seeing Daniel on the video call. So, he was sure it was Daniel only who received the cash from him.

He contacted him and he found Daniel's phone was switched off. He grew apprehensive.

'Had the kidnapper cheated me after receiving the cash? Is he going to free Bhagi or not? Why has he not called me as promised? Why has he switched off the phone? Have I done something wrong by not taking the support of the police?'

Daulat perspired with acute stress when more time lapsed without a phone call from Daniel.

7.45 P.M.

Daulat was losing patience.

His blood pressure shot up. He rushed to a conclusion, in desperation, if he did not receive a call from the kidnapper in the next five minutes, he would go to the police station and file a case.

Before leaving the flat more than forty minutes ago, Daulat promised Sneha that he would bring Bhagi home in twenty minutes. Sneha noticed Daulat carrying one crore cash with him.

'What should I tell Sneha now?' he began worrying.

The phone was ringing.

Expectantly, he looked at the screen. It was not a WhatsApp call from Daniel. It was a call from Sneha.

He guessed she was contacting him to enquire about the fate of Bhagi. He had no answer for the question! He did not respond to the call.

Sneha called a second time. Daulat had not responded.

There was a WhatsApp message from Sneha.

"*Great news! Bhagi is found. Payal called me and said Noel found Bhagi. Where are you? I'm calling you to inform you of this sweet news. Payal is on the way to our flat along with Bhagi. Please call back!*"

Daulat was dumbstruck. He felt a surge of happiness as well as consternation within himself. '*How come Bhagi was found by Noel?*' He got confused.

He called Sneha and exclaimed, "A lovely news it is! Bhagi is found?! I'm coming home in a moment."

7.40 P.M.

Sankar's police van entered Tapaswi Home. Noel and Bhagi got out of the car.

The boys at the orphanage gathered around Noel with bundles of compliments.

Sankar and Payal were briefed by Rama Sastry about the finding of a gunny bag with one crore cash by Jaggu at the dump yard!

Sankar said passionately, "I'm inspired to meet honest people like Rama Sastry, Jaggu and Noel. It's ironic that such honest people are struggling to lead a normal life."

He turned to Payal and said in a firm voice, "Payal, you're in a hurry to take Bhagi and reunite him with his parents. Of course, that's natural on your part. I want your brother Daulat to come here, apologise to Rama Sastry and give an undertaking that he will never seek Rama Sastry to vacate the Tapaswi Home. Then only, Bhagi shall be handed over to Daulat."

Payal knew Sankar was right. She stared down.

She texted Sneha, '*Bhagi is at Tapaswi Home. You come along with Daulat and take him.*'

Rama Sastry curiously asked, "Has Noel found Bhagi? Where?"

"We dropped Aditya and Sandhya at Aditya's house. We were on our way to Tapaswi Home. We were on the Madhapur highway," Sankar narrated. "We were about to cross the lane of Bhagi's school! For a brief moment, the headlights of the van flashed on a small physique. It was Noel who noticed who was that physique! He shouted gleefully, "Bhagi! Bhagi! There is Bhagi!!" We halted the van.

"I peeked in the direction where Noel was pointing his index finger. On our right side, I watched a boy standing under the dark shades of trees. It was the school premises of Bhagi. He stood sobbing in that darkness! Noel went down and brought Bhagi. There was no one around. Payal was ecstatic when she found her nephew. She immediately contacted her sister-in-law and informed her. She requested me to turn the van to Sahiti complex to hand over Bhagi to her brother. I objected. I brought him here and handed Bhagi to you."

"Who left Bhagi in that darkness at the school?" Rama Sastry wondered.

"Daulat shall know it better. Let him come here and divulge what happened. If he does not cooperate yet, I will not let him touch Bhagi!" Sankar was furious.

A Benz car zapped into the premises of Tapaswi Home.

Sneha dashed out of the car, she ran toward Bhagi, hugged her son and wept inconsolably. Daulat saw Bhagi and was exuberant with joy. *Idly* leapt at Bhagi. It rollicked chirpily with its front legs in the air.

Sankar was unhappy. He felt doomed. He had not liked the kind of reunion happening between Bhagi and his parents in front of him.

He wished Daulat should come to know of the generous deeds of Sastry, Jaggu and Noel. He wished the whole episode of re-union should unfold as an eye-opener to Daulat. He coveted Daulat should apologise to Rama Sastry, Noel and Payal.

But, the kind of reunion that was happening in front of him with Daulat not being aware of the noble acts of Rama Sastry, Noel and Jaggu had been annoying him.

An idea struck him.

He hauled the gunny bag with one crore cash that was found by Jaggu. He stormed toward the Benz car and bolted the bonnet with the gunny bag. A huge noise erupted.

Daulat looked up. He saw the gunny bag! His eyes flashed. The crumpled gunny bag with Lord Balaji logo!!

He shouted insanely, "My Cash! My Bag! My Cash! My Bag! My 2000 currency notes!" He ran towards the bag and tried to swoop on it.

Sankar heaved the bag back into his control. He questioned Daulat," How do you know there is cash in the bag?"

Daulat narrated the incident of failed attempt to exchange ransom amount with the kidnapper and he losing that amount on the 25th afternoon in the lane behind the GMC Mall. He inquisitively questioned, "How did this bag reach you?"

Sankar showed Jaggu and clarified, "His name is Jaggu. The boy is an orphan living with Sastry.

"He is a rag picker. He found your bag in the dump yard.

"Daulat! Can you believe, Jaggu has not touched a single rupee! He handed it to Sastry!

"Look at Sastry's gesture. He remembered that it were you who took the gunny bag from the Tapaswi Home. He guessed the cash could be yours. He requested me to hand the cash over to you!!

"One more gift to you, Daulat!

"Your son was found at the school in the dark. It was Noel who had spotted your son.

"You kicked Noel out of your flat. Noel had pardoned the treatment he received at your hands. He had no grudge on you.

"When he saw Bhagi, he jubilantly cried, 'Bhagi! There is Bhagi!' What a kind heart Noel has!

"Had he decided to settle scores with you, had he not cautioned, the van would have moved ahead. Bhagi would have lost himself in that wilderness."

Daulat stood perplexed! He was not able to believe his eyes and ears!

"Daulat, I'm sure you know who abandoned Bhagi at the school!" Sankar commanded. "It's good for you to divulge!"

Daulat felt abashed. He conceded, "Yes. The kidnapper received another one crore from me today less than an hour ago. He said he would drop my son at some unknown location and inform me. I was waiting for his call. But it's not known to me why he has not contacted me after dropping Bhagi at the school?"

"What does he look like? Do you know where he resides?"

"He wears a different outfit every time. Today, he came like a priest on a scooter and collected cash from me." Daulat confessed.

Bhagi was overhearing their discussion with wide eyes. He said excitedly, "Yes, uncle has dressed like a priest today."

"Do you know where his house is?" Sankar asked Bhagi.

Bhagi shook his head in negation. "It's a flat. I don't know where it is. It's a nice flat on the top floor."

"Who else is there in the flat?" Sankar questioned.

"No one else has been there except me and my uncle. We played video games nonstop. Uncle wears a different dress everyday. One day he is a doctor. One day he is like a movie hero. Another day he is a priest. Lots of photos of Gods are there. Beads and brass pots which my grandma possessed in our flat are there. He brought a lot of cash to the flat a while ago." Bhagi recalled fluently.

'Priest dress! Brass pots!' Payal screamed, "Sankar! I know where the kidnapper is! Let's go!"

Sankar handed over the cash bag to Daulat. He cynically asked him to count the cash.

"Sankar! Don't embarrass me anymore!" Daulat confessed, "I'm feeling ashamed! My apologies to Rama Sastry, Noel, Jaggu and Payal!"

Sneha thanked Noel. She pleaded with him to stay in their flat and be part of Payal's project.

Daulat walked up to Rama Sastry. He bent and touched his feet!! He promised Sastry, "Sir! The plot is yours forever!"

He turned to Payal and Sankar and said, "It's my pleasure I will soon conduct your marriage! It's my promise!"

8 P.M.

Daniel was in an ecstatic mood in his flat. The operation went on smoothly. No blood stains! No gunshots! No hot chases! He appreciated himself for his scrupulous planning. He looked at the bundles of cash lying on the table. His joy knew no bounds!

Of all, he liked the anti-climax that he had not anticipated. He mind spooled the incident.

'After receiving ransom money from Daulat at the Shiva temple, I brought cash to my flat. I randomly checked the cash and was satisfied. I decided to leave Bhagi at his school and inform his dad. I started from my flat along with Bhagi on the scooter at 7.30 p.m.

I rode circuitously through lanes to confuse Bhagi. He should not remember the route.

We reached the highway. On the opposite side, there was the lane leading to the school.

Bhagi screeched, "Uncle, why have you brought me to my school? I will not go to school now!"

I told him, "Your dad is on the way to receive you!"

I was about to enter the school lane.

I spotted a police van coming with strobe lights flashing on its roof top.

I got scared.

It did not require much analysis for the police if they happened to see me along with a kid. It would be suicidal to me.

I left Bhagi in the dark alley amidst trees in front of his school. I had no time to tie him to a tree. I had no time to call Daulat and inform him. I left Bhagi at the school.

I turned the scooter around. I crossed the road and disappeared into the lane where I came from.

I realised it would be unsafe to drive a scooter on the empty roads. If the police chose to pursue me, it would be a death knell to me.

I looked around.

I found a safe corner to hide the vehicle for the moment. I shoved the scooter into a dark corner.

Opposite me, it was a two-storey building. I could see shops on the ground floor and the first floor. All the shops were closed. There was no trace of humans.

I could see the staircase on one side. I raced to the open terrace.

I lay prone on the floor, crawled up to the parapet fortification and lifted my head above it. I looked in the direction of the school lane. The distance was around three hundred metres.

The police van stopped. A boy got off the van. He guided Bhagi into the van. The police van left.

Initially, I was puzzled.

Soon, it dawned on me, Bhagi fell into the safe hands of the police. The police would come to know the particulars of Bhagi without any difficulty.

Of course, Daulat would agonisingly struggle for some more time, unable to figure out where his son was!

He would curse me. He might think I was a cheat.

I thought, I should not call Daulat anymore!

I was sure Daulat would soon meet Bhagi in a police station.

I threw the SIM card into the gutter.

I walked fast by foot to the flat. I left the scooter in that dark corner. I wanted to continue to mislead the police. The finding of the scooter at the spot would be a wrong clue to them.

They will be searching for me tomorrow in the wrong places. It helps me to elude them.'

Daniel opened his eyes and felt consummated. He had excitedly touched the bundles of cash spread on the table. He hugged the cash bundles!

One kidnap a year was the motto! One crore a year was the target! He achieved it.

He thought he would use the money for the purpose it was intended for. He updated Vijay Bhaskar, his friend and guru, on WhatsApp about the successful closure of the mission. He promised him a party at a five-star hotel soon!

He decided to abandon the flat. He prepared to shift his camp to a five-star hotel by next morning.

Previous day, he checked with the Hotel Taj and sought a reservation. The Manager notified they were open to accept the new guests subject to medical check-up formalities stipulated by the government in the wake of Coronavirus.

He said it was fine. He confirmed to the Hotel staff, he would reach the Hotel early in the morning.

*****

Providence had a distinct script. It executed its plan more precisely than a million Daniels!

8.10 P.M.

Payal entered the apartment complex of Daniel along with Sankar.

She straightway went to Venkata Swamy's flat and knocked on the door.

When Venkata Swamy appeared, she said to him that she was inclined to seek more Holy brass pots with the Ganges water. She sought the flat number of the gentleman she met previously!

Venkata Swamy greeted Payal and felt happy for the service he could render. He offered to personally come to show Rama Rao's (alias Daniel) apartment!

*****

The doorbell rang!

Daniel shuddered! '*Who has come at this hour?*' He felt nervous.

He glanced through the peephole view of the door!

Venkata Swamy stood there. Daniel looked sideways. No one else was there!

He looked at himself. He was in the priest's costume.

He scampered to the table, gathered the cash bundles in his hands, dumped them into the washing machine and rushed back hurriedly to the door.

He took a deep breath, opened the door with a large grin on his face and said, "Oh! Welcome Venkataswamy…."

Daniel had not yet completed the sentence.

He was perplexed to see an Inspector of Police with a revolver in his hand!

Daniel was stupefied!

Sankar had put the gun on Daniel's head at point blank range!

Venkata Swamy was taken aback!

After a brief search in the flat, Payal found the cash of one crore in the washing machine!

Sankar arrested Daniel!

He searched the pockets of Daniel and pulled out a leather purse. He flipped the folders of the purse. He saw a passport size photo. He was taken aback! He looked at Daniel and questioned him," Who is the boy in this photo?"

"It's me!"

Sankar stared at Daniel and asked, "Who is that old man beside you?"

"He is my mentor!"

Sankar showed the photo to Payal. She was taken aback. She questioned Daniel, "How do you know that old man?"

"I was around 15 years old. I lived like a vagabond. My father passed away. I used to roam in the twin cities," Daniel narrated. "One day, I saw an old man on the footpath in an unconscious state. I admitted him to the hospital. He was given treatment and he survived. He was a retired teacher and widower. He had no children. He learnt I was an orphan. He got inspired to start an orphanage and I was the first orphan to join his home. A dozen more orphan boys soon joined the home.

"I experienced for the first time a sense of family life, a sense of brotherhood and a sense of amiable social life. I loved the ambience. We used to get up in the morning. Did physical exercise followed by prayer and studies! The old man guided the orphans to a better way of life. His name was Rama Sastry! He found it difficult to manage the home with the little money at his disposal. We approached many for donations and did not get help.

"We used to starve without food. I thought I should contribute. I knew only one skill. I used to contribute to the expenditure by indulging in thievery and gold chain snatching etc. He saw me one day doing a robbery. He shunted me out of the Tapaswi Home. I begged and pleaded with him.

"He beat me and asked me to leave the Home. It was a painful experience for me. I have indescribable respect for Rama Sastry.

"I continued my network with a five-year-old boy by name Bharath who himself is an orphan at the Home and continued to help the Home without being noticed by Sastry.

"Recently, Bharath informed me that Daulat Ram, a wealthy person, was pressuring Sastry to vacate the plot. I decided to kidnap his son and demand a ransom. I thought that money would help Sastry to relocate.

"Initially, I thought I would demand the plot itself as ransom. In such a case, Daulat will easily conclude it is Rama Sastry who planned the kidnap. It will land Rama Sastry into more problems.

"This one crore is meant to be delivered to Sastry as if it were donated by multiple donors! It will help him to relocate the Home to a new place. I'm sad I'm caught before I can accomplish my goal!"

Sankar and Payal listened to him awestruck. The photo had the image of a boy and a sixty-year-old man! They remembered Rama Sastry informing them about a boy as his saviour who rescued him when he fell on the footpath and went unconscious! A copy of the same photo was often seen by Payal and Sankar in the photo frames hanging on the walls of Tapaswi Home! They realised now that the old man in that photo was Rama Sastry and the boy was Daniel!

Payal said, "Daniel! You achieved your goal. Daulat is my brother. One hour ago, he donated the plot to Rama Sastry forever!"

Daniel's face brightened with joy!

Sankar arrested Daniel and moved him to the police station! He seized one crore cash, phone and leather purse of Daniel.

A while ago, when Payal and Sankar were searching the flat, Daniel managed to send a WhatsApp message to Vijaya Bhaskar that he was arrested by Madhapur police!

By the time all formalities of arrest were over, it was 11 p.m.

Sankar said to Payal, "Rama Sastry is to be informed tomorrow morning about Daniel!"

Chapter 22

DANIEL ESCAPED FROM THE JAIL

Next day at 11 a.m. Sankar was at the Tapaswi Home and he apprised Rama Sastry about the previous night incident of arrest of Daniel.

Rama Sastry could not believe that Daniel had continued to support his cause all these years. Initially he was reluctant to meet Daniel. Sankar persuaded him and both went to the police station.

When they entered the police station, they had come to know that Daniel was not in police custody.

The Station House Officer informed Sankar, "Sir! Daniel reported 'Coronavirus positive' and we've just moved him with escort to Gandhi Hospital for treatment."

Sankar suspected foul play.

Daniel was kept in the cell at 10 p.m. last night. He looked healthy! 'How can he be tested 'positive' in a day?' Sankar suspected. He verified the records and found that the station sent samples of three inmates to the lab while they received four test reports.

Lab technician was caught and he confessed to having added the fourth report pressurised by a person who came to the Lab in the early morning at 7 a.m.

It was Vijaya Bhaskar who managed the fourth report.

Sankar drove fast to Gandhi Hospital accompanied by Rama Sastry.

Vijaya Bhaskar was already at the Gandhi hospital in the uniform of a male nurse to help Daniel escape from the hospital.

A police constable sat outside the "Corona' Ward as security. Vijaya Bhaskar had come to the Ward in a nurse uniform. He brought a wheelchair. Daniel sat in the wheelchair and he was carted out of the Ward.

Bhaskar had taken Daniel in the wheelchair from Ward to Ward through the corridors of Gandhi Hospital. When they reached an isolated corner, Daniel removed the patient wardrobes and wore a trouser and shirt brought by Bhaskar. Both began to walk out of the Hospital toward the Car parking.

Sankar's police van arrived at the hospital. Sankar suggested Sastry stay in the police van and he scampered toward the Corona Ward. He saw Daniel fleeing and chased him.

Daniel and Vijaya Bhaskar also saw Sankar and they managed to flee, sneaking through the multiple rooms of the hospital.

They reached the car parking.

Daniel saw Rama Sastry in the police van. He walked over to him and with folded hands he said, "Sir! I learnt Daulat gave away the plot to the Home forever! I'm happy.

"I've decided to start a new lease of life. I'm going back to Kakinada to take up Church Services as my vocation. Bharath has my phone number. In case of need, please contact me. I don't hesitate to take on anyone in case you're in trouble!" He touched the feet of Rama Sastry. He rushed toward the car where Vijaya Bhaskar was waiting. They fled in the car in a flash of a second.

Sankar arrived at the car parking place after thirty minutes. He was gasping. He said, "Daniel is hiding somewhere in the hospital! I've instructed my team to search each room in the hospital!" He asked the security staff of the hospital to close the exit and entry gates!

Rama Sastry didn't inform Sankar that Daniel met him a while ago before he fled! Sastry was in a contemplative mood whether to help Daniel pursue his new lease of life or divulge the truth to Sankar and get him arrested! He had two disciples in two distinct walks of life!

Sastry kept quiet!

*****

Five years passed. The twin cities had developed multifold. Global MNCs had been opening their offices in the prime areas of the city.

One of the biggest hotel chains in the world approached Daulat. They offered Rs. 100 crores toward the plot where Tapaswi Home was. Daulat could not resist the temptation. Greed and wealth won over Daulat once again!

He knew Rama Sastry would not be able to seek the support of Sankar and Payal as before!

Sankar and Payal were married. Sankar was promoted as SP and he was posted at a district headquarters place far away from Hyderabad. Payal was very busy with production and distribution of music albums! Noel was a star now!

Daulat met Rama Sastry and warned him to vacate the plot! Rama Sastry was now 80 years old!

Rama Sastry had not informed the latest threat of Daulat to Sankar and Payal.

He contacted Daniel!!

Daniel reincarnated to rescue his mentor! He took out the '*Daniel attire*'- a jeans trouser, a T-shirt and a leather jacket-from his wardrobe once again and took the flight from Rajahmundry to Hyderabad the same day to take on Daulat!

Daniel thought he should take over the management of Tapaswi Home in order to bury the threat of Daulat Ram forever and also give relief to his ageing mentor-Rama Sastry!

He remembered the quotation of his friend Vijaya Bhaskar. Vijaya Bhaskar predicted five years ago itself that

Daulat would surely lay his hand on the plot once again one day! He quoted, ***"Greed of the rich breeds crime! And crime is a necessary evil!"***

THE END

www.ingramcontent.com/pod-product-compliance
Lightning Source LLC
LaVergne TN
LVHW041207150826
845673LV00001B/319

* 9 7 9 8 8 8 8 6 9 9 6 0 7 *